Praise

"Prabhu Dayal's delightful book about his years in our Karachi Consulate 1982-85 covers a gamut of subjects including Pakistan's nuclear programme, US arms assistance, Kashmir, the Punjab problem, Zia's Islamisation policies, movies, the plight of minorities, religious and ethnic violence and of course cricket. Written in a breezy, anecdotal style, the book entertains even as it illuminates. More than a memoir, a genuinely instructive read about a vital period in India-Pakistan relations."

Dr Shashi Tharoor, M.P.

Prabhu Dayal was a young, bright and enthusiastic diplomat, who joined me in my early days as Consul General Karachi in 1982. We then lived in interesting times. Pakistan was slowly, but surely, changing from being a relatively liberal country with a vibrant civil society, to a more conservative religious orientation, under the dictatorship of President Zia ul Haq.

Prabhu's book provides a highly readable, enjoyable and perceptive insight into the times when Scotch Whiskey flowed freely in evening parties, in a city that was later to sadly become a hotbed of ethnic and sectarian tensions and violence".

Ambassador G Parthasarathy

"Prabhu Dayal handles the recounting and analysis of the Pakistan political climate during the years 1982- 1985 with great insight and storytelling skills and presents a perspicacious analysis of the socio-political situation during that period. He handles the subject with elan and keeps you glued to the book till the last page'.

Ambassador Shashank, former Foreign Secretary

We learn from history. Prabhu Dayal in his book takes the reader through the labyrinth of Pakistani politics and its society during the 3 years from 1982-1985 when he was posted at India's Karachi Consulate. This book attempts to pull the India -Pakistan relationship from the quagmire in which it is today.

Bhaskar Ghose, former Secretary to the Government of India

KARACHI HALWA

Prabhu Dayal

Illustrations by Chandini Dayal

ZORBA BOOKS

Published in India by Zorba Books, 2015

Website: www.zorbabooks.com
Email: info@zorbabooks.com

Copyright © Prabhu Dayal

ISBN 978-93-85020-32-2

Zorba Books Pvt. Ltd.(opc)
Gurgaon, INDIA

Printed in India

Dedicated to my Twins

Akansha and Akshay

For Kashif
From
Ashfaq Uncle
EID-UL-FITR
2022

Dream on!

Prologue

It was the second half of 1981, and my tenure as Second Secretary at the Indian Embassy in Cairo was coming to an end. The three and a half years that I had spent in the Egyptian capital were a highly rewarding experience for a debutant in the complex world of international diplomacy.

Soon after my arrival in Cairo, Egypt and Israel had signed the *Camp David Accords* in September 1978, which paved the way for the Peace Treaty signed in March 1979. In recognition of this momentous achievement, President Sadat and Prime Minister Begin were jointly awarded the Nobel Peace Prize for that year. In his acceptance speech, Sadat had said, "Let us put an end to wars, let us reshape life on the basis of solid equity and truth."

This Peace Treaty ended the state of war that had existed between Egypt and Israel since 1948. It made Egypt the first Arab country to recognise Israel, but for the same reason it became unpopular in most of the other Arab countries. In their view, Sadat had betrayed the concept of Arab unity, and Egypt was suspended from the Arab League in 1979.

In short, it was a period of hectic diplomatic activity. I was on my toes all the time trying to cope with the tasks assigned to me. As a result, I was now looking for a good break. It was no secret to my colleagues at the Embassy that I was sure that I would soon be winging my way towards Europe or America for

..ext posting. I started daydreaming about all those wonderful places I might be headed to.

On one such day, a colleague walked into my office with a broad grin on his face and a telex message in his hand.

"Great news!" he proclaimed.

Trembling with excitement, I asked him: "Washington? London?"

His grin was so broad that I was sure it had to be one of these.

He handed me the telex – in those days e-mails or even fax messages had not yet arrived on the scene, and all good and bad tidings were sent by the External Affairs Ministry by telex.

"KARACHI?" I screamed in disbelief, while his grin grew even broader. Not even in my worst nightmares had I seen myself being packed off to Karachi from Cairo.

I had every reason to believe that the Pakistanis would be hostile to me. Our two countries had fought wars in 1948, 1965 and 1971, respectively, and in the last amongst these, we had achieved a decisive victory that resulted in the creation of Bangladesh.

I was miserable at the thought of being sent off on a posting to a country where I was sure to be regarded as an enemy.

I stayed in Cairo for a few weeks more, agonising each day over how fate had dealt me such a cruel blow. I was so dejected that I could well have sat down to write my own obituary.

There was, however nothing else I could do about it.

Omar Khayyam's famous verse would often come to my mind:

The moving finger writes, and having writ,
Moves on; nor all thy piety nor wit
Can lure it back to cancel half a line
Nor all thy tears wash out a word of it.

While briefly in Delhi *en route* from Cairo to Karachi, I received a message from Additional Secretary SK Singh asking me to see him. It was his 'moving finger' that had decided to send me to Karachi, for he was the all-powerful head of administration at the Ministry of External Affairs. Some years later, he would become the Foreign Secretary and move his finger with even greater authority to decide the fate of his colleagues – including the most senior ones.

"We are sending you to a challenging assignment," he told me. I interpreted this to mean that it was an assignment for which there were no takers.

Throughout our meeting, it was quite evident that he was just trying to cheer me up and boost my morale.

We had a chat about Karachi and the tasks for the Consulate. In a lighter vein, he remarked: "I love Karachi *halwa*. It's delicious, though it often gives me indigestion."

Halwa is an Arabic word meaning a dessert or sweet that is generally flour or nut based. The dessert itself has been adopted by many cuisines, which have introduced their own variations, and *halwa* is now part of the lexicon of many languages. The Indian subcontinent is home to many different types of *halwa* too, but Karachi *halwa* is a highly regarded and well-liked speciality.

Though I embarked on my stint in Karachi with little enthusiasm, the three and a half years I spent there turned out to be unforgettable in several respects and fill me with nostalgia even today, after the passage of three decades.

My diplomatic career has taken me to several continents, but I must admit that in no other country did I feel such an overpowering sense of a common heritage as I did in Pakistan. In both countries, the issues in focus are those that divide us. This is of course, unfortunate since present-day India and Pakistan have existed under similar influences for millennia and have remarkable similarities in a number of areas such as language, literature, art and architecture.

I found that there was something rather unique about the experience of living amidst my colonial cousins. The warmth and affection that I sometimes received there remain etched in my memory.

One occasion that I remember fondly was when I wanted to buy a camel-skin lamp and found a shop that had just what I wanted. As I was paying the bill, the elderly shopkeeper somehow figured out that I was from India, and asked me which city I hailed from. When I told him that I was from Allahabad, he refused to take any money from me as his wife was also from there! Finally, he agreed to let me pay, as long as I would accept two lamps for the price of one!

During my stay in Karachi, I met several people who were the very embodiment of sophistication and refinement. Remnants of the legendary *nawabi* era, they were a charming blend of wealth and culture – poignant reminders of an age fast receding into the past.

There were also many enchanting evenings I spent at spellbinding concerts of Pakistani maestros, or at *mushairas* (Urdu poetic symposia) graced by the participation of renowned Pakistani poets. I felt truly enriched by such cultural fiestas.

Then there were those equally enjoyable evenings that I spent just relaxing in the company of a few close Pakistani friends. Such occasions gave me the opportunity to savour the best of Karachi humour – always original, though at times somewhat cynical.

These and many other memories fill me with sweetness even today.

On the other hand, I was often witness to the unabashed lying and duplicity that Pakistani leaders have developed into a fine art. Their pronouncements were often at such variance with ground realities that they were difficult to digest.

My posting in Pakistan turned out to be so much like Karachi *Halwa*!

Mightier than the mighty

I

Karachi, located on the Arabian Sea coastline is the capital of the Sindh province of Pakistan. It is Pakistan's largest and most populous city.

When I lived there in the early Eighties, the population of the city was around 9 million, which has today grown to over 15 million. The population of Greater Metro Karachi stands at a staggering 25 million making it the most populous city in the Islamic world.

This gigantic metropolis reputedly started as a small fishing village established by settlers from Baluchistan and the Makran coast. Legend says that an old fisherwoman Mai Kolachi (*Mai* means a senior and respected lady and Kolachi was her tribe) along with her community settled in the Indus valley delta. Named Kolachi after them, the settlement gradually grew into a bustling port. There is a locality in Karachi that is still called Mai Kolachi. Interestingly, the name Karachi was first used in a Dutch document in 1742 when a merchant vessel was shipwrecked near it.

Karachi was the capital of Pakistan till 1958. The capital was shifted that year to Rawalpindi and later on to Islamabad. However, Karachi's importance did not really diminish as it remained Pakistan's leading financial centre as well as its main seaport and industrial hub.

The people of Karachi considered their city to be the liveliest in the country, even more so than Lahore. Many of them would dismiss the sparkling capital city of Islamabad as being a soulless place.

There was a joke that someone from Karachi won a week's free stay in Islamabad as the first prize in a raffle. He actually requested the organisers to give him the second prize because he couldn't bear the thought of spending a whole week in boring Islamabad, only to discover to his horror that the second prize was a two-week free stay in Islamabad!

The demographic structure of Karachi is rather interesting. Although Karachi is the capital of Sindh, the Sindhis themselves constitute only around 7% of its population. Punjabis make up 16% of the population, while the Pathans and Balochis make up 11.5% and 4.5%, respectively. *Muhajirs* are its largest constituent and make up more than 60% of the population.

Muhajir is a term used to describe immigrants and their descendants who migrated from different regions of India at the time of partition, that most bloody event in the history of the subcontinent which witnessed the killing of an estimated half a million people. Around 7.3 million Hindus and Sikhs moved to India from Pakistan, while around 7.2 million Muslims did so from India to Pakistan in what was the biggest population transfer in history.

Most of the immigrants from India who hailed from the region of present-day Punjab, Haryana and Himachal Pradesh settled in Pakistan's Punjab province, while those who came from the British Raj Provinces of Bombay, United Provinces, Central Provinces, Bihar and elsewhere, settled down mainly in Karachi and some other cities of Sindh, such as Hyderabad, Sukkur and Mirpur Khas.

During my numerous interactions with various Sindhis in Karachi, I noticed how these facts relating to the city's demographic composition rankled them.

In a city with such a high percentage of *Muhajirs*, the Indian Consulate was bound to have a high degree of relevance and importance. The *Muhajirs* had relatives in India—parents, siblings, in-laws, uncles and aunts—whom they wanted to visit from time to time.

The Karachi Consulate's jurisdiction also covered the provinces of Sindh and Baluchistan and included many other cities, such as Hyderabad and Nawabshah which had a sizeable population of *Muhajirs* too. Thus, the pressure on the Consulate's visa section was bound to be extremely high at all times, as I was to discover in no time.

I served under two Consuls General— Mani Shankar Aiyar followed by G. Parthasarathy—both of whom ranked among the best Foreign Service Officers of their generation. Later, Mani left the Foreign Service and entered politics going on to become a Cabinet Minister in the Manmohan Singh government, while Partha rose to the highest echelons of the Foreign Service and held several important assignments, including that of High Commissioner to Pakistan. They provided an inspiring leadership to their colleagues in the Consulate and made extraordinary efforts to build a broad-based relationship with Pakistan. It was a great learning experience and a privilege to serve under them both.

When it comes to dealing with Pakistan, Mani is perceived as a dove while Partha is seen as a hawk. However, these labels had not yet been affixed on them when they were heading the Karachi Consulate in the 1980s. They were both considered top notch diplomats endowed with incredible energy, intellect and commitment to their professional responsibilities.

K. Natwar Singh was the Indian Ambassador in Islamabad at that time. Considered very powerful in the Foreign Service community and a brilliant public speaker, he was also highly respected in Pakistani intellectual circles.

One anecdote always comes to my mind when I think of those days.

Ambassador Natwar Singh and his wife had come on a visit to Karachi, and wanted to buy some table tops made from onyx, the beautiful green marble for which Pakistan is so famous. We went to several showrooms, but Mrs. Singh did not like any of the pieces shown to her. Getting a bit tired of going from showroom to showroom, the Ambassador pointed to a few table tops remarking that they were 'very nice' and that they should just buy them.

Mrs. Singh snapped at him: "Natwar, you don't listen!" To which he replied with a shrug: "What else do I do?" It was difficult but I somehow managed to control myself from laughing out loud. Even the mighty Ambassador Natwar Singh was no different from most of us!

Mir Jafar, the wretched traitor!

II

The Indian Consulate General is located on Fatima Jinnah Road, named after the sister of Mohammad Ali Jinnah, the founder of Pakistan. Located less than half a mile down the same road is the Flagstaff House. Although Jinnah owned this building, he had never lived there himself. However, after his death, Fatima Jinnah moved in and lived there till 1964. The building was later acquired by the Pakistan Government and converted into a museum depicting Jinnah's life. It is one of the most important heritage buildings in Karachi and is now called *Quaid-e-Azam House*.

Jinnah is greatly revered in Pakistan as *Quaid e Azam*, which means 'Great Leader'. This title has also been bestowed by their respective countries on China's Mao Zedong as well as North Korea's Kim Il- Sung, Kim Jong-Il and Kim Jong-un.

Another landmark was the Sind Club. Situated just a stone's throw away from our Consulate, this club had the highest snob value in Karachi. It continues to use the British colonial spelling 'Sind' even though the province is spelt as 'Sindh' after independence.

The Sind Club had been set up for the Colonialists, and natives were not allowed into it. It was only in 1952 that a few Pakistanis were admitted as members. A Pakistani was allowed to become its President only as late as 1965! Women were not allowed into the club, except for the Ladies Dinner held every two months and for the Club's Annual Dinner. The club actually had a sign saying 'Women and dogs not allowed'! This was removed only after independence.

Incidentally, Iskander Mirza was among the first Pakistanis to be admitted as a member of the Sind Club in 1952. He was the last Governor General of Pakistan from 1955-56 and subsequently, the first President of the country when the Constitution was promulgated in 1956. He was also the great grandson of Mir Jafar, also known as 'Mir Jafar the Wretched Traitor', whom the British made the Nawab of Bengal after they had defeated Siraj ud Daula. Mir Jafar was a puppet of the British East India Company and is someone who is reviled in India, Pakistan and Bangladesh. Pakistan's national poet Allama Iqbal described Mir Jafar as 'a disgrace to the faith, a disgrace to the nation and a disgrace to the country'. In Urdu, the term *Mir Jafar* is used in the same sense as *quisling* is used in English!

Yet, it was the same Mir Jafar whose great grandson became the first President of Pakistan! As someone cynically remarked, "What a torchbearer! Imagine what blood flows in his veins!"

Situated next door to the Consulate was the mansion of the Haroon family, descendants of Sir Abdullah Haroon who had been one of Jinnah's closest associates. Having piloted the *Independence of Pakistan Resolution* in the Sindh Provincial Muslim League Conference at Karachi in 1938, he had been regarded as a very important leader of the Muslim League.

Sir Abdullah Haroon's younger son Mahmood Haroon was Interior Minister of Pakistan at that time, while his grandson

Hameed Haroon was running *The Dawn*, Pakistan's most prestigious newspaper. Another grandson, Hussain Haroon was active in Sindh politics, but was far better known in his capacity as President of the Sind Club. Later on, he would serve as Pakistan's representative to the UN during the Zardari government and was regarded by everyone who knew him in New York as a perfect gentleman. The Haroon family was held in the highest esteem not just in Karachi, but elsewhere in Pakistan too.

The Pak-American Cultural Centre and the British Council were located across the road from the Indian Consulate.

However, even though there were many important landmarks in the vicinity, the hustle and bustle in this neighbourhood was always centred round the Indian Consulate, which had huge crowds of visa seekers thronging to it all day long.

The residence of the Indian Consul General was located at 63, Clifton, across the road from 70 Clifton, better known as Bhutto House. Clifton was the most affluent area of Karachi and housed many of the rich and powerful. In recent years, Clifton has gained notoriety because Dawood Ibrahim, India's most wanted terrorist who has been given sanctuary in Pakistan, is believed to be living in Clifton.

A posse of policemen was deployed at the entrance of the Consul General's residence, not only to provide security to him, but also to keep an eye on visitors entering and leaving Bhutto House when Benazir Bhutto was being kept under house arrest there.

The Indian Government owned three other compounds which were used for the residences of other officers and staff members. These were thoughtfully named Hindustan Court, Panchsheel Court and Shivaji Court, respectively. Over 50 families who resided there valued the security afforded by togetherness. Life in Karachi could be violent and unpredictable at that time and has become much more so over the years.

The Indian government acquired these building complexes with sprawling compounds to set up the High Commission since Karachi was the capital of Pakistan when it came into existence in 1947. However, the capital was shifted to Rawalpindi in 1958 and later on to Islamabad, and the High Commission also moved there. The Consulate had a well-equipped auditorium and massive lawns where hundreds of invitees could attend events. However, the variety of restrictions imposed by the Government of the Islamic Republic of Pakistan (especially on dance and music) meant that we could utilise these facilities only to a very limited extent.

The Consulate was closed in 1994, and all these buildings are lying completely unutilised. It is doubtful that the Consulate will be reopened anytime soon. An inspection of these buildings some years ago showed that they had been vandalised and many of the movable items had been taken away by 'thieves', even though the premises are guarded by the police.

+ + +

Even the toothy smile could not conceal.......

III

Karachi winters are usually mild, but there was a cold wave when I landed there in December as it had snowed a day earlier in Quetta. Whatever happens in Quetta, the effects are always felt in Karachi as well as in many other places in Pakistan.

However, much more chilling was the Martial Law that had been in force in Pakistan since July 1977 when General Muhammad Zia ul Haq staged a coup, deposed the elected Prime Minister Zulfiqar Ali Bhutto, became Chief Martial Law Administrator and subsequently, President.

Zia had Bhutto executed in April 1979 and arrested his daughter, Benazir as well as several other political leaders who opposed him.

Naturally, Zia was feared by the common man in Pakistan. After he assumed power, people did not take long to figure out how wily and deceitful a person he was; nothing that he said was to be taken at face value. Zia's eyes reflected his steely determination as well as his ruthlessness. Even his toothy smile could not camouflage this aspect of his character.

But Zia could be a real charmer whenever he wanted. KB Lal, the renowned civil servant and diplomat, once narrated an anecdote that illustrates Zia's tremendous public-relations skills.

When Zia overthrew Bhutto and became President, people came to know from a press release that he had studied at the famous St. Stephen's College in Delhi. Since none of his contemporaries had any recollection of him, they reached out to Professor Kapadia, who was considered a walking encyclopaedia on all matters pertaining to St Stephens. He just could not recall anyone by the name of Zia-ul-Haq. Even when shown a group photograph, Prof. Kapadia was unable to do so. When someone pointed to a boy in the last row, Professor Kapadia pondered awhile and then nodded, perhaps it was Zia, but he couldn't be sure. On being asked how Zia had been as a student, Prof. Kapadia replied, "Ordinary sort of fellow…" in a somewhat dismissive manner.

Some years later, a group of teachers and students from St. Stephens College, which included Professor Kapadia, visited Pakistan at Zia's invitation. Not only did Zia host a dinner for them at his residence, he himself came down to the portico to receive them. All through the dinner, he showered the guests with utmost affection and attention and was particularly warm towards Prof. Kapadia, whom he repeatedly referred to as his old history teacher. All this completely bowled over the Professor, and in subsequent years whenever someone asked him what Zia-ul-Haq was like in his college days, his reply had changed to: "Brightest boy in the class!"

Zia-ul-Haq was born into a lower middle class family in August 1924 in Jalandhar, India. His father was a clerk in the British Indian Army. Zia studied in Simla and then went to St. Stephens College. He joined the British Indian Army in 1943 and fought in the Second World War in Burma. In 1947, he joined the newly formed Pakistan Army and served as a tank commander in the Indo-Pak War of 1965.

Zia was stationed in Jordan from 1967-70 as a Brigadier and helped to train King Hussein's forces. Significantly, he led the Jordanian troops he was training into battle during the *Black September* operations against the Palestinians.

Black September was a conflict between the PLO led by Yasser Arafat and the native Jordanians led by King Hussein. Thousands of people, mainly Palestinians, were killed in the fighting. The Jordanian army triumphed and this helped the King to remain in power. Zia won King Hussein's gratitude, but became a hated figure for the Palestinians.

On his return to Pakistan, he was promoted to Major General and then Lieutenant General.

My Pakistani friends told me how in the race towards the top, he managed to steal a march on his peers, who were completely outsmarted by this wily fox. He was commanding the 2nd Strike Corps at Multan when he invited Prime Minister Bhutto for an official visit. As part of the preparations, he got his tailor to stitch a Ceremonial Military uniform for Bhutto.

The Prime Minister was very pleased at being asked to dress in this military attire because he liked pomp and ceremony. He was also made to climb atop a tank and shoot a target, which was duly hit. Bhutto was thrilled as he thought that he himself had hit the target, but in reality it was hit by someone else from another tank!

Knowing Bhutto's over-sized ego, Zia had devised this ingenious method of flattery!

Zia also reportedly made it a point to meet Bhutto privately and pledge his loyalty to him.

Sure enough, a few months later, Bhutto controversially appointed General Zia ul Haq as Chief of Army Staff superseding as many as seven more senior officers. He trusted Zia and believed that he was religious and non-political. According to Pakistani sources, the Americans also lobbied for Zia because they found him more acceptable than other officers senior to him.

The wily and scheming Zia had carried the day and stolen a march on the others. The rest is history.

In later years, Nawaz Sharif would make a similar mistake as Bhutto had made. Whoever said that learning from history is easy?

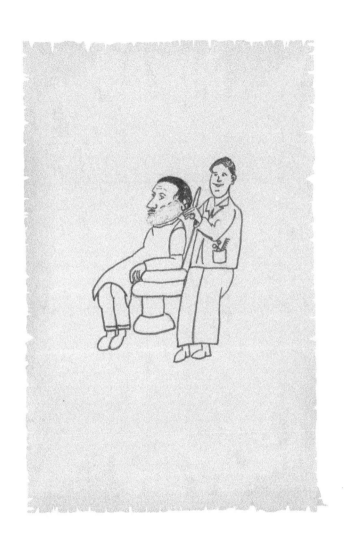

The art of shaving

IV

Just after staging the coup against Bhutto on 5th July 1977, Zia appeared on national television and said: "My sole aim is to hold free and fair elections which will be held in October this year. Soon after the polls, power will be transferred to the elected representatives of the people. I give a solemn assurance that I will not deviate from this schedule."

Years passed but Zia kept dragging his feet on the issue of holding elections. He was completely insincere about his solemn promise to the nation and kept postponing the elections on some pretext or another.

The joke summing up the popular cynicism doing the rounds in Karachi is worth recalling.

Zia's barber would come to shave him every morning. While shaving, the barber would ask him, "Sir, when are you going to hold the elections?"

Zia would just parry the question and reply, "After some time."

One day Zia got irritated with the barber for asking him the same question about elections every day. "You're just a barber, not a politician," he said rudely. "Why do you keep asking when I will hold the elections?"

To this the barber replied coolly: "Sir, I'm not really concerned about this matter – but whenever I mention the word 'elections', your hair stands up and I find it easier to give you a shave!"

I heard this joke at several Pakistani gatherings, and on each occasion everyone would burst into raucous laughter. It was a pointer to what they really thought about their President's promise.

Although Zia had given a solemn assurance about handing over power to elected representatives within 90 days of the coup, he had no intention whatsoever of actually doing so. Like many other military dictators, he spoke of the indiscipline which accompanies a multi-party parliamentary democracy. He preferred the Presidential system, with decisions being made by a handpicked team. Zia's team comprised mainly serving and retired military officers, retired bureaucrats and technocrats.

Zia ruled as only a dictator would. Civilian authority was completely subjugated by him, and Martial Law Administrators were put in charge at every level. Zia himself was the Chief Martial Law Administrator till he took over the office of the President of the country on 16 September 1978.

Although many opportunistic civilians also began to range themselves alongside him, his real support base was the army.

Zia disbanded the Parliament in 1979 and replaced it with the Majlis Shoora, which was merely a consultative council to advise him on the process of Islamisation.

The members of the Majlis were not elected, but appointed by Zia. Their job was to merely endorse his decisions. He nominated all the ministers of the Federal Government too. Among the people he appointed were Agha Shahi as Foreign

Minister. A career diplomat, Shahi had served as Foreign Secretary under Bhutto. Zia also appointed the well-known World Bank economist Dr. Mahbubul Haq as Finance Minister.

In similar fashion, Zia (or his Governors) appointed all the Provincial Ministers. Naturally, most such appointees regarded Zia as their political godfather. It may be mentioned that Pakistan's current Prime Minister Nawaz Sharif also made his debut in the political arena with Zia's blessings.

Under Zia's dispensation, a search was launched for new urban leaders willing to serve under the Martial Law regime and Nawaz Sharif was hand-picked to be the Finance Minister of Punjab province. A corporate tycoon and owner of a steel mill, he had been devastated by Bhutto's nationalisation policies. His entry into politics was believed to have been on account of the need to get back his business. Not unexpectedly, as Finance Minister of Punjab he piloted the denationalisation legislation and got back his steel mill.

Later, with Zia's support, Nawaz Sharif became the Chief Minister of Punjab province and acquitted himself well in this important role. Given the preponderance of the Punjab province in Pakistani politics, it was widely believed that in the coming days he would play an important role in national-level politics – and this turned out to be true. When he assumed power on the national stage, he completely reversed Bhutto's nationalisation policies and ushered in other policies based on economic liberalisation.

Thus, the unabated hostility between the Bhutto family and Nawaz Sharif had its origins in the nationalisation of Sharif's steel mill. Had this nationalisation not taken place, Nawaz Sharif may well have focussed his attention only on his business and perhaps not found it necessary to enter politics. It was a classic case of adversity turning into opportunity.

Pakistani politics is a bumpy ride. It is ironic that Nawaz Sharif pitted himself against Bhutto and alongside the coup-stager General Zia – only to be ousted later when he himself was the elected Prime Minister by another coup-stager, General Musharraf!

Up above the world so high, I am a General in the sky

V

Zia was able to sideline the political parties and keep Pakistan under martial law due to the backing of the army.

A lot has already been spoken and written about the pivotal role the army plays in Pakistan. It is the final arbiter in politics and perhaps, everything else. However, there is some check on the army's privileges when there is a civilian government in Pakistan. Under Zia's Martial Law Regime, there were hardly any checks and the army's power was absolute.

Zia created a system wherein his fellow officers stood to gain a lot if he continued in power. Officers of the armed forces enjoyed power and pelf which they were loath to let go and therefore, supported him to the hilt unconditionally.

Zia made sure that in virtually every sphere it was the army that ruled the roost. Generals close to him were appointed Provincial Governors, administering martial law in their respective jurisdictions. There were also Martial Law Administrators at every level who often rode roughshod over the civilian officials.

Being from a country such as India where the army never oversteps its role, I found the situation in Pakistan not just strange, but also tragic. I was witness to how civilian authority was being systematically humiliated, crushed and demoralised.

Zia enhanced the army's stake in the corporate sector significantly. The *Fauji Foundation*, a corporate organisation run by the army, was expanded considerably during his tenure. It became one of the largest corporate groups in Pakistan. Naturally, all the plum positions went to senior Generals who were loyal to Zia. It was cronyism of a sort which I could never have imagined earlier.

Not just the politicians, but many other people were unhappy with the army's encroachment on civilian authority. The army was seen to have generated unprecedented material benefits for itself, a fact which became a source of resentment among the common people. This was most visible in the real estate sector.

There was a new vigour with which Defence Housing Societies were developed, and army officers got large plots of land at throwaway prices. Many Pakistanis felt that the army was misusing its position while also getting distracted from its actual role and functions. I heard a joke on this in a Pakistani gathering, which reflected the widespread cynicism about what was going on.

Generals from various countries were sent up in a rocket to orbit around the planet. They were given telescopes to see what was happening on planet Earth. The American quickly found a nice location for himself and was soon looking intently into his telescope. When asked what he was looking at, he replied that he was looking at the places the Soviet troops were concentrated in.

The Russian who was also peering into his telescope, explained that he was observing the build-up of the NATO troops. The Indian said he was looking at the borders of China and Pakistan to see their troop deployments. Similarly, all the Generals explained what they were looking at.

The Pakistani General was by himself in one corner, looking intently into his telescope. When the others around him asked whether he was studying the Soviet deployments in Afghanistan or the positions of the Indian troops across the border, he replied nonchalantly, "I'm trying to see which corner plots are available in Lahore's Defence Housing Society."

A man is as good as his word

VI

Zia was invariably at his charming best with foreigners, especially the Americans. However, as regards his own countrymen, he ruled over them with an iron fist. I recall how the common man in Pakistan did not trust him, but ironically the US did. The Reagan administration bestowed legitimacy on him, though the Americans are always the most vocal and fervent champions of democracy and human rights.

Not just Pakistani politicians, but even some American analysts were disappointed at their government's support to Zia. How could they reconcile such support with the avowed US position on ushering in democracy all around the globe and championing human rights everywhere?

It was a classic case of the application of the medieval jurist Henry de Bracton's maxim: "That which is otherwise not lawful is made lawful by necessity." The US Government's perception of Zia was coloured by the fact that it considered him to be a necessary player in their efforts to dislodge the Soviets from Afghanistan.

Zia was a frontline ally in the US-led war against the Soviets. It did not matter much to the Reagan Administration that he was nothing but a usurper who had deposed a lawfully elected Prime Minister and executed him. The Americans did not really care beyond a point whether Pakistan was reeling under martial law, or that its jails were filled with politicians opposing the military junta. What mattered to them most was the support Zia lent them in their efforts to try and push the Soviets out of Afghanistan. They wanted to retain this support at all costs, and Zia knew this as well as anyone else.

The net result was that the Reagan Administration armed Pakistan to the teeth on the plea that the latter needed such weapons to face off the Soviets in Afghanistan. We were deeply dismayed as we had absolutely no doubt that all this weaponry would be used not against the Soviets, but against us.

It has been very aptly said that a gun that fires in only one direction is yet to be invented. The American weapons given to Pakistan and meant for bolstering its defences against the Soviets on its western border ultimately ended up enhancing its offensive capability against India on its eastern border.

Reagan's predecessor, President Carter had initially cut off aid to Pakistan as there had been no progress in the discussions on the nuclear issue. However, after the Soviets invaded Afghanistan in December 1979, President Carter offered Pakistan $350 million as aid over three years. Zia famously rejected this offer as 'peanuts'. He had sensed that Carter was on the way out, and played his cards very shrewdly.

Under Reagan, the US-Pak interaction grew by leaps and bounds, with the CIA and the ISI working closely together. The ground was laid for US military aid to flow to Pakistan as never before. Soon, a $3.2 billion aid package spread over six years was signed and a separate arrangement was made for the supply of 40 F-16 fighter aircraft.

In a move that showed lack of foresight as well as a bias against India, the Americans subjected us to nuclear sanctions, but at the same time looked the other way whilst Pakistan pursued its avowed goal of developing a nuclear bomb. It was amazing that Pakistan was allowed to pursue a nuclear programme which everyone knew was weapons-oriented from its very inception.

Prime Minister Bhutto had said that the Pakistanis would 'eat grass' till they made the 'Islamic bomb'.

President Zia made sure that the Pakistanis didn't need to 'eat grass' as American largesse flowed quite generously into their country.

Pakistan's 'Islamic nuclear bomb' programme proceeded unimpeded despite international concerns. On the basis of Zia's false assurances, the Reagan Administration continued to certify year after year to the US Congress that Pakistan was not developing a nuclear bomb so that weapons supplies to it could continue unhindered. It was the Administration's view that such supplies were essential for the Afghan resistance.

US Government records, which were declassified later, show that the Reagan Administration was aware that Zia was lying to them about his country's nuclear programme, but they allowed such concerns to be overridden by their diplomatic interests in Afghanistan.[1]

These documents also prove that US Intelligence agencies had provided Reagan with evidence to show that Pakistan was relentlessly pursuing a nuclear weapons programme, and that the White House feared that if these intelligence reports became public, it would become difficult to continue military and economic aid to Pakistan.

I cannot forget how experts not just in India, but elsewhere too would hold their heads in disbelief over Washington's indifference to the dangers posed by Pakistan's nuclear programme. A conclusion drawn in many academic and political circles was that Pakistan was let off the hook because of the belief that its nuclear weapons programme was India-specific, and that it would pose a threat only to India.

Did the US authorities really believe that Zia was telling the truth when he repeatedly told them that he was not pursuing a nuclear weapons programme? This was not the case at all. They were quite aware that he was lying to them. This is evident from the secret cable (now declassified) which Vernon Walters, Deputy Head of the CIA sent after the meeting he had with President Zia.

During this meeting he conveyed to Zia that the US had incontrovertible information that the Pakistanis or people purporting to represent them had sent designs and specifications of nuclear weapons components to agents in several countries for the purpose of having such components manufactured for Pakistan. In absolute denial mode, President Zia said that these designs could not have been submitted to foreign agents without his knowledge, and that he had no knowledge about such a weapons development programme. Zia also gave his word that Pakistan would not develop, much less explode a nuclear weapon or device. Walters commented in his cable 'Either he really does not know, or he is the most superb and patriotic liar I have ever met'.[2] It is inconceivable that Zia did not know what was going on, which leaves one in no doubt about what Walters thought about him.

The tragic fact is that by choosing to overlook the intelligence reports about Pakistan's nuclear weapons programme, the Reagan Administration ended up creating a Frankenstein.

The US policy towards Pakistan's weapon's oriented nuclear programme was in sharp contrast with its recent hardline stand on Iran's nuclear programme. Iran was subjected to crippling sanctions. Pakistan's efforts to become a nuclear weapon state could have been held in check by the Reagan Administration. Unfortunately, this did not happen, and soon it was too late to put the genie back into the bottle.

Unlike the prevalent wisdom of the early 1980s, when Pakistan's nuclear weapons were seen as a threat to India alone, there is a much more rational evaluation of the situation today. Evidence that has come tumbling out points to the fact that Pakistan and its nuclear czar AQ Khan had been selling nuclear weapons technology and components to North Korea, Iran and Libya. Former Iranian President Rafsanjani has himself revealed in a recent interview that his country had received nuclear technology from Pakistan through AQ Khan, who believed that the Islamic countries had to have a nuclear bomb.

The rapidly evolving situation in Pakistan has sent alarm bells ringing all around the world. Pakistan is witnessing a continuous surge in extremist Islamic radical groups, which could in turn be inching ever closer to the nuclear trigger. Pakistan's army, the largest among the Islamic countries is not unaffected by the surge of Islamic radicalism which applauds *jihad* (holy war against infidels) and *shahadat* (martyrdom). The fact that this army is laden with nuclear weapons creates a frightening situation for much of the world.

In this day and age, when suicide bombings and mass killings are becoming so common, there is the looming spectre of misguided *jihadis* (ISIS, Al Qaeda, Taliban, Lashkar-e-Taiba, Jaish-e-Muhammad or whatever such organisations they belong to) managing to get hold of nuclear weapons from Pakistan's massive arsenal. They could unleash apocalyptic disaster while sacrificing their own lives in the belief that they are taking the expressway to paradise to claim their prize of beautiful virgins, for this is what they are taught. Fanaticism and religious indoctrination have reached incredible dimensions in Pakistan, and nothing can be ruled out as impossible.

Mango Tango

VII

Zia also launched a charm offensive against Indians. One Indian leader whom Zia was able to win over completely by his guile, was Morarji Desai.

Zia had ousted Bhutto in a coup in July 1977 only four months after Desai himself became Prime Minister of India. Both had a strong dislike of Indira Gandhi, and this fact drew them close to each other. After his coup, Zia was looking for legitimacy for his military regime, as also for stability in foreign relations. He reached out to Morarji who was completely taken for a ride by his public relations skills.

Zia used to call Morarji his elder brother and flatter him. According to the late B Raman, who was Additional Secretary in RAW (India's Intelligence agency), Zia used to telephone Morarji from time to time giving the impression that he was keen on practising urine therapy.[3]

Zia knew fully well that Morarji was not only an ardent follower of this therapy, but was also keen to propagate it to others. Zia would ask him all sorts of questions about urine therapy, such as whether the first urine of the morning should be drunk or a later one, how many times it should be drunk, etc. etc. His frequent telephone calls completely won Morarji over.

Subsequently, Morarji revealed to Zia what India knew about Pakistan's bomb-making facility at Kahuta and shared the information collected by the Indian intelligence agency RAW in this regard. It is understood that Morarji had a pathological hatred for RAW, which he mistakenly saw as an agency created by Indira Gandhi to be used against the opposition parties.

Zia immediately took action to make Kahuta impregnable in case of external attack. He also destroyed the RAW network in Pakistan which had been carefully built up over years of painstaking efforts.

Incidentally, this was not the only favour Morarji did to Zia and to Pakistan's nuclear weapons programme. It is understood that when the Israelis wanted refuelling permission for the aircraft they were going to use to attack the Kahuta nuclear facility, Morarji refused to grant this permission.

It is not surprising that Zia nominated Morarji for Pakistan's highest civilian award, the *Nishan-e-Pakistan*. However, before this award could be conferred, Zia was killed in a plane crash in 1988. Benazir Bhutto, who became Prime Minister then, refused to give the award to Morarji as she believed that he had done nothing to save her father from the gallows. Later, when Zia's protégé Nawaz Sharif became Prime Minister, the award was finally conferred on the nonagenarian Morarji at a private ceremony at his home in Bombay in May 1990 because he was too old to travel to Pakistan.

Queen Elizabeth (1960), President Tito and President Eisenhower (both in 1961), President Nixon (1969), Nepal's

King Birendra and Prince Karim Aga Khan (both in 1983) were the only foreigners on whom the award had been conferred before it was given to Morarji. No other Indian has been conferred this award given for 'the highest degree of service' to Pakistan'.

Without doubt, Morarji had rendered 'the highest degree of service' to Pakistan!

The following year, Morarji was conferred the *Bharat Ratna*, India's highest civilian award. This made him the only person to have received the highest civilian awards from both India and Pakistan. However, in view of the 'highest degree of service' to Pakistan outlined above, one wonders if the *Bharat Ratna* should have been conferred on him.

Incidentally, many others were taken in by Zia's charm offensive—even the Soviets did so briefly. When Zia went to Moscow to attend Brezhnev's funeral in 1982, he met with the new Secretary General Andropov who expressed his anger at Pakistan's covert involvement in the Afghan resistance against the Soviet Union. Zia affectionately took Andropov's hand and told him, "Mr. Secretary General, believe me, Pakistan wants nothing but good and healthy relations with the Soviet Union." [4] Andropov believed him, but soon discovered that Zia was lying through his teeth, and that in reality he was deeply involved in the American efforts to push the Soviet Union out of Afghanistan.

Unlike Morarji Desai, Indira Gandhi did not trust Zia at all, although she did play along when he pursued mango diplomacy with her. Both would send each other many local varieties of mangoes to sweeten the relationship.

Interestingly, Sri Lanka's Prime Minister Sirimavo Bandaranaike snubbed Zia and refused to accept the crate of juicy mangoes he sent through the Pakistan Embassy. According to an article on Pakistan's mango diplomacy by Dr. Ranga Kalansooriya, she sent them back with a note addressed to the Ambassador which said "Thank you for sending me these mangoes on behalf of President Zia ul Haq. However, I cannot accept a gift from a person whose hands have the blood of Pakistan's elected Prime Minister Zulfiqar Ali Bhutto on them….Please return this gift to the sender".

The article goes on to say, "This was, besides being an unusual diplomatic response, a stinging rebuke to a military dictator who had turned down three appeals by Mrs. Bandaranaike to spare the life of Bhutto and send him into exile. She had even offered to host Bhutto in exile in Colombo". [5]

Unbeatable!

VIII

Pressure continued to mount on Zia to hold elections, both nationally and internationally, and even his American benefactors were finding the situation a bit awkward. Therefore, Zia decided to first secure his own position. He used a devious method to get himself officially anointed as President of Pakistan by holding a referendum on 19 December 1984. Voters were asked whether they supported Zia's proposals for amending laws in accordance with the *Quran* and the *Sunnah*, whether they wanted this process to continue and whether they supported the Islamic ideology of Pakistan. Zia put forward the far-fetched logic that an affirmative vote on these three issues would mean that the people wanted him to continue as the President, though this was not an issue directly addressed by the referendum.

When I visited some areas of Karachi with my colleagues, I saw that the voter turnout was quite poor. Independent observers said that not more than 10% had voted in the referendum. Most Pakistanis stayed away as they believed that the referendum was a farce. However, the government claimed that the turnout had been 60%, and that 95% had cast a 'Yes' vote!

Thereafter, it was announced that Zia had been elected as President by 95%!

Soon afterwards, an interesting joke began to do the rounds.

One of Zia's friends from another country was contesting for the office of President, and he asked Zia for help. He told Zia that he too wanted such a stunning victory.

Zia said: "No problem. I will send my election staff to your country."

So Zia's election staff was sent and the elections were held.

When his staff returned to Pakistan, Zia asked them: "How did things go?"

"They went just fine, Mr. President," they replied.

Zia asked: "95%?"

They said: "Yes, 95%."

He asked "My friend won?"

They replied "How could he win? You won, Mr. President."

Need one say anything more about an election machinery that was created to produce only one result—95% for Zia?

After securing his position through such a farcical referendum, Zia finally agreed to hold general elections to elect the members of the National Assembly, though on a non-party basis. These elections were finally held in February 1985.

The major political parties had asked their members to boycott the elections, but a closer scrutiny of the winners' list indicated that many of the newly elected Members of the National Assembly were in fact erstwhile party adherents! Clearly, they had flouted the instructions of their respective party leaders.

This was neither the first nor the last time that rank opportunism would raise its ugly head as a *sine qua non* of Pakistan's politics. Pakistani politicians do not like to like to be left out in the cold and quickly tend to gravitate towards the power centre.

Zia appointed a low profile Sindhi, Mohammad Khan Junejo as his Prime Minister. However, before handing over power to the new government and lifting martial law, he got the National Assembly to retroactively accept all his actions of the past eight years including his 1977 coup against Bhutto!

When he seized power in 1977, Zia had promised to hand over power to the elected representatives of the people within three months, but he took almost eight years to actually do so. A political analyst in Karachi remarked that these eight long years had turned back the clock for the democratic process in Pakistan not just by eight years but in fact, by eight decades.

Democracy in Pakistan is still struggling to stand on its feet while the country continues to slide towards chaos, becoming more and more a failed state. Sadly, instead of addressing the country's own serious problems such as sectarianism, civil strife and grinding poverty, its politicians and generals seem to be obsessed with Jammu and Kashmir, which they want to snatch away from India. This was as true during Zia's rule as it has been before and after.

Please fix my TV

IX

Sultan Ahmad, the eminent columnist of *The Dawn* newspaper, and someone who was regarded as the doyen of Pakistani journalists in Karachi told me a very interesting story.

One night, someone rang up President Zia and said: "Mr. President, my TV has a problem. Please fix it."

Zia was furious and told the caller: "How dare you call me for this sort of nonsense? Take your TV to a mechanic."

Caller: "Sir, I have shown it to several mechanics and they have all told me that only you can fix it."

Zia: "Take it to the Pakistan TV office. I will tell them to look at it."

Caller: "I had taken it there, but even they told me the same thing – only the President can fix it."

Intrigued, Zia asked: "What is wrong with your TV?"

The caller said: "A *mullah* has got inside it and he refuses to come out."

This was not just a wonderful example of Pakistani humour, it was also a reflection of the prevalent mood of cynicism about how Zia was forcefully enforcing Islamic practices in the country after coming to power. He had adopted a policy of Islamic conservatism as the primary plank of his military government.

Zulfiqar Ali Bhutto had already tried to stem the tide of street Islamisation by making concessions to the Islamist parties. For example, he had banned the drinking or selling of alcohol by Muslims. He had also banned activities such as gambling and horse racing.

Zia went much further, vowing to enforce *Nizam-e-Mustafa*, an Islamic system with *Sharia* law (as opposed to Pakistan's predominantly secular laws inherited from the British). He declared that "Pakistan was created in the name of Islam and will continue to survive only if it sticks to Islam. That is why I consider the introduction of an Islamic system as an essential pre-requisite for the country".

A lot has been written in the international media about the *madrasas* or traditional religious schools in Pakistan, but it needs to be underlined that they received state sponsorship for the first time under Zia. During his rule, their number grew over three and a half times from 893 to 2801.The *madrasas* fanned the flames of hatred not only against non-Muslims, but also towards other Muslim sects. They provided free religious training as well as room and board to impoverished Pakistanis who were made to undergo intensive indoctrination.

How much Zia was motivated by piety and how much by political calculations is debatable. However, what is undeniable is that he shouldered a great deal of responsibility for Pakistan's steady and alarming slide into radicalism and Islamic extremism. Intolerance in some sections of Pakistani society grew exponentially on account of Zia's policies. Tragically, it has now become a part of the warp and woof of Pakistan.

Nusrat Bhutto, the wife of the executed Prime Minister said that Zia insanely used Islam to ensure the survival of his own regime.[6]

The official media was utilised by Zia for propagating Islamisation. Islamic preachers or *mullahs* appeared on television to deliver long lectures on Islam lasting several hours. How true it was that the *mullah* had got inside the TV and was refusing to come out!

The most well-known Islamic *mullah* to appear on Pakistan TV was Dr. Israr Ahmed. His rise and the events leading to his eventual exit as reported in the media make a very interesting story. Known to be a proponent of the idea of the modern-day Islamic Caliphate, he had been handpicked by President Zia, who probably felt that these ideas would lend support to his own dictatorship as he too was ushering in Islamic values and systems.

Dr. Israr Ahmed would speak on religious matters to audiences assembled in the television studios. Soon, his lectures also began to touch upon social, moral and political issues. He began to emphasise the Islamic *hijab* for women and would object if any women in the audience did not have their heads covered. His views in this regard were believed to have compelled Pakistan TV authorities to instruct women news readers and anchors to suitably cover their heads and follow the system of *hijab*. These changes did not go unnoticed.

Getting more confident and emboldened, Dr. Israr Ahmed reportedly declared in a TV lecture that he wanted cricket to be banned in the country as it made Pakistanis ignore their religious obligations. He also said that cricket matches should not be shown on TV because Pakistani fast bowlers rubbed the cricket ball on their trousers near their groins in an obscene and suggestive manner, and that this corrupted the minds of young girls! He reportedly singled out Imran Khan in this regard. "Our mothers' sisters and wives watch all this on TV and in the cricket stadiums," he said, while demanding that women should not be allowed entry into cricket stadiums.

The media reported that he was miffed that this lecture was not telecast and practically ended his association with Pakistan TV after this. Reportedly, even though some attempts were made to persuade him come back, these were unsuccessful as he insisted that the episode containing his views on cricket and its corrupting influence on women be aired as a pre-condition for his delivering any more lectures. This was not accepted by the concerned authorities.

This entire episode was covered by the Pakistani media at that time and has been recounted in detail by the brilliant Pakistani columnist Nadeem Paracha.[7]

President Zia's late night caller must have been relieved that at least this *mullah* exited from his TV set!

Some time ago, a Pakistani friend who lives in New York expressed his admiration about how India had put in place a system to nurture talent, and how in the global corporate arena, Indians have done well and have gone on to become the CEOs of some of the world's leading organisations. He mentioned the names of Sunder Pichai (Google), Satya Nadella (Microsoft), Indira Nooyi (Pepsico), Rajeev Suri (Nokia), Anshu Jain (Deutsche Bank) and Ajay Banga (Master Card), though the list includes several others too. He then went on to lament that thanks to Zia-ul-Haq, Pakistan's youth today can only aspire to become CEOs of organisations like the Taliban, Al Qaida, Lashkar-e-Taiba, Jaish-e-Muhammad and others of this ilk. He quipped that it wouldn't surprise him if a Pakistani were to soon become CEO of the Islamic State!

Dracula!

X

Besides a whole host of other things, even film songs were banned on Pakistan TV as part of Zia's hardline Islamisation policies. I remember how Pakistanis often said that they had stopped watching TV as it had become too boring.

So what were they watching instead? Pirated Bollywood movies, of course! Video cassettes of the latest Bollywood movies were smuggled into Pakistan from Dubai and were widely available in Karachi. Sometimes my Pakistani friends would brag about how they saw Indian movies even before they were released in India! Needless to say, there was a huge demand for video cassette players and every Pakistani returning from abroad was sure to bring one home.

Conversations in social gatherings often turned to gossip about Bombay's tinsel town. Normally not a film buff, even I started glancing through every issue of *Filmfare* and *Stardust* in order to impress the lovely ladies of Karachi who were more interested in Indian cinema stars than in the twists and turns of Indo-Pak relations!

Sadly, even before Zia's rule, the Pakistani authorities had not allowed Bollywood movies to be shown in their movie halls. The Lollywood movies (movies made in Lahore) that were shown did not attract many viewers as they were poorly made, had hackneyed themes and were no patch on the grand Bollywood blockbusters. Cinema houses in Pakistan could run such movies for only a few days unlike Bollywood movies that ran for weeks in India.

Nonetheless, Pakistan did have a film industry which churned out a fairly decent number of films (albeit of a poor quality) under Zulfiqar Ali Bhutto. When Zia seized power from Bhutto, he dealt a crushing blow to Lollywood. In 1979, he banned all Pakistani films that had been made in the previous three years. The Motion Picture Ordinance (1979) promulgated by Zia placed severe restrictions on filmmakers. The Islamisation policies he adopted did not spare the film industry –dancing and romantic scenes were not allowed by the censors.

The Pakistani film industry went into a rapid decline, and cinema houses started shutting down and getting converted into shopping malls. Zia has been criticised for the great damage he did to the Pakistani film industry. Some critics feel that he was trying to please the Saudis. Riyadh and Islamabad were the only two world capitals at that time not to have a cinema house, and they have retained this unique distinction.

After Zia, the Pakistani film industry made an effort to revive itself, but the crippling blow that it had been dealt made it difficult. The huge difference between the standards of Indian and Pakistani films remains even today – if anything, it has only increased.

In our conversations, Pakistanis would lament about how their film talent did not get adequate opportunities to realise their true potential due to government policies. Thankfully, Bollywood has helped out. If Pakistanis like Salma Agha, Javed

Shaikh, Fawad Khan, Humaira Mallick, Rahat Fateh Ali Khan or Adnan Sami have got the international adulation they so richly deserve, it is only because Bollywood provided them the necessary platform to do so.

While on the subject of films, I cannot help but recall the seething anger which seemed to have gripped Pakistan when Richard Attenborough's 1982 film *Gandhi* was released. The international acclaim the film received was in sharp contrast to the way people in Pakistan reacted to it. The film was not screened in movie theatres anywhere in Pakistan, though many people did manage to see it as its video cassettes were available.

I had several screenings of the film at my home for small groups of my Pakistani friends, some of whom appreciated it and said so quite openly. However, the widespread feeling in Pakistan was that Jinnah had been negatively portrayed in the film as someone who was responsible for a lot of bloodshed as he was hell-bent on the partition of India. There was also severe criticism of the choice of Alyque Padamsee for the role of Jinnah. People were not happy that Jinnah was shown as a scowling villain throughout the movie.

In response, the Pakistani authorities decided to commission a film on Jinnah with the objective of portraying him as a much greater leader than Gandhi, as also to highlight the fact that Pakistan was founded as an Islamic state (to give greater credence to Zia's Islamisation policies). Titled *Stand Up from the Dust*, the film was never released on account of its poor quality.

Later in 1998, another film on Jinnah was commissioned by Farooq Leghari, who was Pakistan's President at that time. However, this film also drew criticism in Pakistan on account of the fact that Hollywood actor Christopher Lee was cast in the title role of Jinnah.[8] Lee was famous for having played the role of Dracula in several films, and people associated him only too strongly with the image of a vampire, blood dripping from his mouth! There were protests all over Pakistan, and Christopher Lee also reportedly received death threats. Throughout the shooting of the film, he was surrounded by armed guards! Even though the Pakistan Government withdrew its funding half way through the production, the film was somehow completed.

The film had a scene in which a Muslim extremist attempts to attack Jinnah for supporting women and minorities, calling him a traitor. Jinnah tells him that he is an ignorant fool, adding: "Islam does not need fanatics like you. Now grow up and serve Pakistan."[8] Obviously, this message did not go down well with many in the Pakistan Government who wanted the adoption of the *Shariat* (Islamic law), and it did not seem to have had any effect on the Islamic extremists in the country.

This film on Jinnah did not achieve even an iota of success as compared to Richard Attenborough's *Gandhi* which was nominated for eleven *Academy Awards*, and won eight, including Best Picture, Best Director and Best Actor.

Ghazal King Mehdi Hassan

XI

The plight of the film industry in Pakistan was symptomatic of the 'cultural oppression' stemming from the restrictions imposed by Zia ul Haq on the freedom of expression. People would often lament that as a result of such restrictions, two of Pakistan's greatest poets, Faiz Ahmed Faiz and Ahmad Faraz had both chosen to go into self-exile rather than live under martial law.

Faiz is undoubtedly one of the greatest poets not just of Pakistan but of Urdu literature itself. This is manifested by the fact that he was nominated for the Nobel Prize for Literature as many as four times. He was also an avowed Marxist and a founder member of the Communist Party of Pakistan, which was later banned in Pakistan.

Faiz was awarded the *Lenin Peace Prize* by the Soviet Union in 1962. His left leanings are all too evident from his poems as also from this extract taken from his acceptance speech at the *Lenin Peace Prize* award ceremony:

Human ingenuity, science and industry have made it possible to provide each one of us everything we need to be comfortable provided these boundless treasures of nature and production are not declared the property of a greedy few, but are used for the benefit of all humanity. However, this is possible only if the foundations of society are based not on greed, exploitation and ownership but on justice, equality, freedom and the welfare of everyone.[9]

Faiz never hesitated to raise his voice against dictatorship in Pakistan. For this, he was imprisoned or detained on the orders of Pakistan's rulers more than once, despite his exalted status as the country's foremost Urdu poet. He was a staunch opponent of the martial law regime of Zia ul Haq and self-exiled himself to Lebanon following Bhutto's execution in 1979.

However, Faiz returned to Pakistan three years later in 1982 due to his deteriorating health and the civil war in Lebanon. I had the privilege of hearing him recite his poems at a small, private gathering in Karachi. He had an endearing presence, but at the same time, his failing health, especially his asthmatic condition was also all too evident. He passed away in 1984.

Ahmed Faraz, who regarded Faiz as his mentor, was another great Pakistani poet who went into self-exile after being arrested by Zia ul Haq's government for criticising martial law. He described Zia's rule as the worst period for Pakistani writers. It may be mentioned that his opposition to military rulers was not limited to Zia ul Haq. Later, in 2004, Faraz was awarded the *Nishan-e-Imtiaz*, one of Pakistan's highest civilian decorations, by the government of Pervez Musharraf but he returned it two years later. While doing so, he said, "My conscience will not forgive me if I remain a silent spectator of the sad happenings around us. The least I can do is to let the dictatorship know where it stands in the eyes of the concerned citizens whose fundamental rights have been taken away." [10]

Despite the restrictions on freedom of expression, I found the literary and cultural life of Karachi to be very enjoyable. I attended countless *mushairas* – gatherings where Urdu poets read out their compositions. Without doubt, the standard of literary works produced by Pakistani writers was of a very high quality.

Perhaps even more enjoyable were the numerous concerts by leading Pakistani singers who would weave poems by these poets into musical magic. It was an unforgettable treat to hear legendary singers, such as Mehdi Hassan, Ghulam Ali and Farida Khanum mellifluously singing the *ghazals* or *nazms* written by Faiz, Faraz and other great Pakistani poets; Ustad Nusrat Fateh Ali Khan singing *qawwalis* in his booming voice; or Abida Parveen rendering Sufi songs in her distinctive style.

Even today, I get nostalgic when I hear recorded versions of Mehdi Hassan's *Ranjish hi sahi* written by Faraz or *Gulon me rang bhare* written by Faiz. To have sat just a few feet away from the maestro while he sang them in a live concert was, of course a completely magical experience.

I regretted that my knowledge of literary Urdu was not quite adequate since I had not studied this language during my school or college days. Before we attained Independence in 1947, Urdu was a part of the syllabus in many parts of India, including my home state of Uttar Pradesh, but after Independence, it was somehow discontinued in most schools as it was mistakenly considered to be the language of the Muslim community. My school curriculum included English, Hindi and Sanskrit, a classical language that has not been a spoken language in India for centuries if not for millennia! According to the 2001 census, of a billion people in the country, only 14,135 people said that Sanskrit was their spoken language as against 52 million who said the same thing for Urdu.

The great Nobel Laureate, Rabindranath Tagore had prayed that his country would awake to that heaven of freedom 'where the world has not been broken up into fragments by narrow domestic walls'. Unfortunately, the narrow walls of prejudice did not take long to come up.

I feel that by discontinuing the study of Urdu in most of our schools, we did a dis-service to ourselves as we voluntarily downgraded and weakened our link with an invaluable part of our heritage. If, like Sanskrit, Urdu was also taught alongside Hindi, generations like mine would have been enriched.

It is still not too late to undo the damage and give Urdu the respect it deserves as part of our heritage. Studying Ghalib or Mir's poetry will not only give us an idea of their incredibly refined intellect, it will also help to increase our understanding of those bygone eras which they so richly depict in their verses.

On my part, I made an active effort to make up for lost time and studied Urdu during my stay in Pakistan. I felt considerably rewarded as I could soon understand and enjoy Urdu poetry and *ghazal* concerts much more than before.

One of the largest and most popular literary gatherings in Karachi at that time was the annual *Indo-Pak Mushaira* at the Indian Consulate. It was a masterstroke of Consul General Parthasarathy, a Tamilian who did not know much Urdu but saw such a gathering of intellectuals as an effective way of building a cultural bridge between the two countries. The Consulate lawn would resonate with applause for hours as top notch Urdu poets from both countries recited their literary compositions, new as well as old. The event would be the talk of the town for weeks on end.

The cocky Musharraf

XII

During my posting in Cairo, I had become acquainted with the Pakistan Military Attache, Col. Ali Kuli Khan Khattak. We often played tennis and occasionally bumped into each other at diplomatic receptions. He was a pleasant fellow, and a good tennis player too. We got along rather well.

He was happy to hear that I had been posted to Karachi, and told me that his father lived there. When I asked for his father's contact details so that I could go and meet him in Karachi, he told me not to worry, for his father would contact me when I got there. Neither did he tell me who his father was, nor what he did.

A few days after my arrival in Karachi, I got a telephone call from General Habibullah Khan. My office told me that he was a former Chief of Staff of the Pakistan Army, and that after leaving the army he had gone into business and become one of the wealthiest persons in Karachi. Gen. Habibullah was the father-in-law of Gauhar Ayub, the son of former President Ayub Khan.

"My son, Ali has written to me about you, and I would like you to come over for lunch." It was only then that I realised that Ali's father was such a powerful and important person in Pakistan! Most people tend to brag about such things, but Ali had not mentioned even a word about how powerful, rich and important his father was! I thought that was real class.

Gen. Habibullah warmly welcomed me to his home, saying "The relations between our two countries will have their ups and downs, but I want you to always feel at home in my house as you are my son's friend." During my numerous visits, he would regale me with stories about his military career, especially the Second World War in which he served in Burma as a captain with the Bihar Regiment. Not surprisingly, he was later invited to India in 1991 by the Bihar Regiment for its Golden Jubilee Celebrations, which, despite his age and health problems, he made it a point to attend.

In due course, Ali Kuli Khan Khattak became the senior-most General in Pakistan and was tipped to be the Army Chief. I felt happy for him. However, Nawaz Sharif superseded him and instead appointed Pervez Musharraf whom he saw as being loyal to him! Ali resigned in protest.

What followed was a traumatic chapter in the history of Pakistan and the sub-continent. Musharraf waged the Kargil War against India, which Ali Kuli Khan has called the biggest tragedy in Pakistan's history, even bigger than the loss of East Pakistan.[11] Musharraf later ousted Nawaz Sharif in a coup and the latter had to spend several years in exile in Saudi Arabia.

No doubt, Zia and Musharraf had many similarities. Both were highly ambitious, scheming and unscrupulous. Both hated India and wanted to harm it. Like other officers from the Pakistan Armed forces, it was perhaps natural for them to do so – they could not forget Pakistan's humiliating defeat in the 1971 war.

However, they were quite different from one another in some vital aspects. Zia was regarded as a deeply religious person unlike Musharraf. More importantly, Zia was shrewd enough to understand that open hostility with India was not a good or correct strategy. India was militarily much more powerful than Pakistan and had routed the latter a few years ago; it would do so again if the occasion arose. On the other hand, the adventurous and cocky Musharraf risked the Kargil war with India in which he suffered a crushing defeat. According to Pakistani sources, the army had given a similar proposal to Zia for an infiltration into the Kargil region, but he had not assented, fearing that an all-out war would not be to Pakistan's advantage.

Zia's strategy towards India was in line with his personality— cunning and sly. He proposed a No War Pact, which drew support from his principal backers, the Americans and the Chinese. However, the Indian Prime Minister Indira Gandhi was a seasoned politician who saw through his game. She had a historical perspective and felt that Pakistan would use such a pact as a cover for its arms procurement programmes. Nobody could forget that the Nazis had signed a No War Pact with the Soviet Union in August 1939, and that Hitler used the pact to his advantage but trashed it less than two years later when he attacked the Soviet Union in June 1941.

The No War Pact offer was a classic ploy by Zia. It was meant to overcome the objections of US Congressmen who were opposed to giving military aid to Pakistan as it fuelled the arms race in the sub-continent. If there was a No War Pact, the Reagan administration would be able to pacify them by arguing that such military aid to Pakistan was just meant to strengthen its forces along the Afghan border and did not pose any danger to India.

Zia's offer of the No War Pact bore an uncanny resemblance to the fable of the wolf in sheep's clothing.[12] Knowing full well that India's economic and military strength was much greater, and that there was no way that Pakistan could win a war against us, Zia based his strategy on destabilising India without going to war. His intention was to tie the hands of our armed forces through a No War Pact while at the same time, wage a proxy war through infiltrators sent across the Line of Control. While the respective armies would be bound by the No War Pact, such infiltrators trained and backed by Pakistan's forces would be passed off as indigenous Kashmiri freedom fighters and would therefore, have a free run of the place.

Indira Gandhi made a counter offer and proposed a Friendship Treaty, which would bind the two countries to find a peaceful solution to all disputes bilaterally. The efforts to incorporate the Pakistani proposal for a No War Pact and the Indian proposal for a Friendship Treaty into a common text did not make any headway. In later years, when Benazir Bhutto was Pakistan's Prime Minister, she made it clear that she was not interested in the No War Pact.

Holy cow!

XIII

Zia abetted separatism not just in Jammu and Kashmir, but also in Punjab. Khalistani leaders were frequent guests of his government, and their provocative statements were invariably played up by Pakistan TV and other sections of the media there.

Those days satellite or cable TV had not yet arrived on the scene, but programmes broadcast by Pakistan TV from Lahore could be watched in the towns and villages across the border in India. The Pakistanis tried their best to influence Sikh public opinion and make it as hostile as possible towards Indira Gandhi's government by distorting news about events in Punjab and concocting falsehoods. This was how a full scale media offensive was launched by Pakistan TV.

The Indian Government despatched Information and Broadcasting Minister HKL Bhagat to Islamabad in July 1984. Zia's government gave him plenty of assurances and also a special gift — a Sahiwal cow. Apparently, before partition, Bhagat's family had lived in Sahiwal in west Punjab, now part of Pakistan. Sahiwal cows are reddish-brown and are famous for their high yield of milk.

The visit was high in terms of promises made but low in terms of actual results. It did precious little to stem the tide of mischief brought on by Pakistan TV, which continued to broadcast inflammatory programmes and do everything possible to fan the flames of separatism among Sikhs. The Pakistan government was part of the problem, and it was perhaps too optimistic to expect it to become part of the solution.

Looking back, perhaps the only concession that the Pakistanis made to Bhagat was to respect his dietary habits. Bhagat was a strict vegetarian, and his hosts served a vegetarian spread to the entire Indian delegation at every meal.

However, a prominent member of Bhagat's delegation was quite upset about being served vegetarian food every day, and I recall him mentioning how he had been looking forward to having those delicious Pakistani kababs but had to settle for potato cutlets instead!

Front page media commentaries in Pakistan continued to gleefully hint at the impending creation of Khalistan. I cannot forget how annoying it used to be to read most Pakistani newspapers, especially the Urdu language ones on account of their false, malicious and mischievous reporting. We had to be on our toes and keep issuing rejoinders, which were carried by the newspapers many days later, and that too, tucked away in some insignificant corner.

After *Operation Blue Star* in June 1984, the Pakistani media shifted into top gear and raised their pitch against India. I can never forget the screaming headlines in the hardline, virulently anti-India Urdu daily *Nawa-i-Waqt*, which quoted Jagjit Singh Chauhan (founder of the Khalistan movement) as saying, "Indira Gandhi will not live to see the sun rise in 1985."

Naturally, when Indira Gandhi was assassinated in October 1984, there was a widespread feeling not just in India, but elsewhere too that the Pakistanis had abetted her assassination.

The Zia government did not confine itself to merely encouraging the Khalistanis. Even more sinister was the fact that Pakistani terrorists in the garb of Sikhs were sent across the border into India to create mayhem. The border was not fenced at that time and several Pakistanis masquerading as Sikh terrorists were shot and killed by our security forces.

"How can your police allege that the terrorists were Pakistanis?" I was often asked.

"By looking at the evidence inside their pants," I would reply, adding, "Sikhs are not circumcised."

In a nutshell, Zia's government did everything possible to abet the Sikh militancy and fan the flames of separatism in Punjab. It even went to the extent of hiring Sikh extremists from Canada and putting them up in gurdwaras at Nankana Sahab and Punja Sahab, respectively. The primary function of these Canadian Sikhs was to attack Indian Embassy officials who were assigned liaison duties to assist the *jathas* (pilgrim groups) which visited these holy shrines. The Pakistani media would then gleefully go to town on how the Sikhs had attacked Indian officials, glossing over the fact that these were their own hirelings.

There was no doubt whatsoever that such brazen attacks repeatedly took place only because of the connivance and full involvement of the Pakistani authorities, who did nothing to nab the culprits. Several of our officials were injured in such shameful incidents – these included my close friends Bhushan Jain, Counsellor, and Ramesh Pandey, First Secretary, as also OP Tandon, my assistant.

Naturally, the attacks caused great annoyance not only in our government, but also among the general public in India. We lodged protests with the Pakistan authorities, but these had no effect whatsoever on them.

One evening, a Pakistani diplomat Tanvir Ahmad was roughed up outside his house in Lajpat Nagar in Delhi. The Pakistanis were quick to blame RAW for the incident, but there was no evidence for this. Thereafter, the physical attacks on our diplomats stopped. Whoever was behind the attack on the Pakistan diplomat was successful in sending out a message that enough was enough.

Crocodile tears

XIV

When Indira Gandhi was assassinated on 31 October 1984, sweets were distributed in many areas of Karachi and other cities in Pakistan, and celebrations were held in many places. It was widely believed that the government and right-wing Islamic parties were behind such despicable acts.

Clearly, her assassination gave great joy to many Pakistanis who saw her as the chief architect of Pakistan's breakup in 1971 and the creation of Bangladesh. I don't recall sweets ever being been distributed in India when any Pakistani leader has died, and hope that it does not happen in the future either.

Zia, who never seemed to run out of crocodile tears, came to attend Indira Gandhi's funeral. A friend of mine at the External Affairs Ministry was attached as Protocol Assistant with the Pakistan delegation. He recounted something that was a huge eye opener for many of us.

The Pakistan delegation along with many others was put up at the Asoka Hotel. When Zia and his entourage returned to the hotel after the funeral, they found that there was already a big queue of people waiting to get into the elevator as several other delegations had also returned around the same time.

Not wanting to wait, Zia said that he would take the stairs. When one of his entourage members tried to dissuade him because his suite was on the fifth floor, Zia said something to him in a low voice, assuming that everyone around him was a Pakistani. He did not realise that one of them was my friend, the Indian protocol official. Indians and the Pakistanis look quite similar, don't we?

You can never imagine what Zia said softly, almost in a whisper.

He said, *"Aaj to hum paanch manzil bhi charh jayenge."* Roughly translated, it means, "Today I will climb even five floors." Such was his sense of elation!

A few days after Indira Gandhi's assassination, I attended a reception in Karachi where I met Brig. AR Siddiqui, a prominent Pakistani military expert and Director General of the Institute for Inter Services Public Relations. He served as the Official Spokesman of the Pakistan armed forces.

Having downed more than a couple of drinks, his tongue loosened up and he said: "Mr. Dayal, very soon you will not be able to recognise the map of your country." Clearly, he was hinting that Punjab was going to break away from India.

I retorted that this would happen only if Pakistan itself ceased to exist as a separate country and re-joined India. He was quite miffed with my reply.

Nonetheless, Brig. Siddiqui's remarks were an indication of how military analysts and strategic thinkers in Pakistan viewed the developments across the border in India. They were quite convinced that India was going to break up as their own country had done a decade earlier. Zia's government had done everything possible to fan the flames of separatism, and people like Brig. Siddiqui were sure that these efforts were going to bear fruit soon. It was not difficult to understand that this was something they were hungering for; they simply wanted revenge for Bangladesh.

Most Pakistanis considered Zia a usurper and regarded the military rule imposed by him as illegitimate. However, when it came to the subject of India, almost everyone seemed to give his policies the stamp of approval.

I got the unmistakeable impression that not just military analysts like Brig. Siddiqui, but most Pakistanis wanted that Bangladesh should be avenged. Although I did come across some Pakistanis from time to time who genuinely wanted good relations with India, the majority did not wish India well, and would not do so in the foreseeable future.

This was the impression I got when I was posted in Karachi in the early Eighties, and it is much the same impression I have today. I am not alone in thinking like this, as countless opinion polls have shown that most Indians share the same pessimism with regard to Pakistan.

East or west, Indian tyres are best!

XV

Pakistan's negative approach towards India would become amply clear whenever we sat down to discuss bilateral trade. I had the opportunity to sit in several meetings with Pakistani delegations as I was handling the commercial portfolio in the Consulate.

We gave Pakistan MFN (Most Favoured Nation) treatment; any item whose import into India was permitted could be imported from Pakistan. On the other hand, the Pakistanis had a list of only 32 items that could be imported from India, and even these items were those that we ourselves were importing from other countries! However, the items which we were in a position to export were not included in Pakistan's list.

Later, their list was grudgingly expanded, but again the expanded list only had items that were of no interest to our exporters as we ourselves were importing them. It needs to be mentioned that Pakistan refuses to give India MFN treatment even today, always offering some excuse or another.

Ironically, this negative approach did not hurt us as much as it hurt Pakistan. Because of their competitiveness, Indian goods still found their way into Pakistan. Smugglers were very active along the border and many Indian items reached Pakistan through them. Interestingly, Indian-made whisky was also among the items that got smuggled in, and brands like Haywards and Black Knight were available at a high premium in Karachi. I often had Indian whisky at Pakistani homes.

More significantly, many Indian products used to be imported by Pakistani companies through Dubai and Singapore, but with the manufacturers' labels changed and 'Made in India' tags removed! Businessmen always find solutions to their problems.

There was a third method by which Indian goods found their way into the Pakistani market. Pakistan had given transit facilities for Indian exports to Afghanistan; Pakistani businessmen in tandem with Afghan importers made sure that many items exported from India to Afghanistan never went beyond Peshawar!

Truck tyres were one such item. I used to be surprised at the fact that Afghanistan was importing such a large quantity of tyres till I understood what was really happening. The tyres were being unloaded in Peshawar itself, and many Pakistani trucks were happily running all around the country on Indian tyres!

Importing through third countries or through smugglers instead of direct imports from India only increased the costs for consumers while depriving the state of revenue through custom duties. But this is not something that the Pakistan authorities were bothered about. It was a classic case of cutting one's nose to spite one's face.

It is not that we didn't try to persuade the Pakistanis to be reasonable. One lasting impression I have of my years in

Karachi is how our government strenuously endeavoured to change the Pakistani mindset, as also to widen and deepen people-to-people contacts.

We nurtured the hope that if Pakistani public opinion became friendlier towards us, then in due course it would be able to influence their government's policy towards India. However, this did not turn out to be the case.

We also promoted contacts in all areas such as culture, sports and films. Pakistani singers such as Mehdi Hasan and Ghulam Ali frequently came to India and charmed our audiences. What was the Pakistan Government's response? It was not willing to permit Indian artistes such as Lata Mangeshkar and Jagjit Singh to perform in Pakistan. The government in Islamabad was as obstructive as it could be. This was consistently their policy under Zia ul Haq, though it changed a bit under later regimes in Pakistan. Eventually, Jagjit Singh and a few other Indian artistes like Sonu Nigam, Daler Mehndi and Mika Singh performed in Pakistan, albeit much less frequently than their Pakistani counterparts perform in India.

This negative approach of Pakistan was equally evident with regard to their general visa policy. The Indo-Pak visa agreement provided for visas for visiting relatives. We liberally gave visas to Pakistanis to travel to India, except if they were on our blacklist (99% Pakistanis were not) as we were keen to promote stronger people-to-people relations. Sometimes, the number of visas issued by the Indian Consulate in Karachi was in excess of 1000 per day! Applicants generally got their visas the day they submitted their applications. On the other hand, Islamabad made it as difficult as it could for Indians wanting to visit Pakistan.

To achieve this objective of issuing the maximum number of visas per day, the Consular staff exerted every sinew, and both Mani and Partha during their respective tenures as Consul General, did everything possible to encourage and exhort each and every team member. They made even the person with the lowest rank feel that he or she was doing an important job that was helping to raise the prestige of the Consulate. It was great captaincy by both of them.

Quite often, I used to be amazed to see how people walking on the streets would stop and wave when the Indian Consul General's car passed by, the Indian flag fluttering on it. Most of these people were *Muhajirs* (migrants from India) or their descendants.

By stopping and waving at the Indian Consul General's car, they conveyed their appreciation for the ease with which they themselves had got their Indian visas, and for the helpful approach of the Indian Consulate. Sometimes when they met us at gatherings, they would open their hearts and tell us that their relatives in India who applied for Pakistani visas faced enormous difficulties in getting the same, and that many of them did not get the visas at all.

Train from Pakistan

XVI

While people could get their Indian visas with ease, travelling from Karachi or elsewhere in Sindh (where the *Muhajir* population was concentrated) to India was difficult and presented tough challenges. Those who could afford to travel by air would reach Delhi or Bombay in a few hours, but the vast majority of the travellers were not so affluent. Often there were several family members travelling together, making air travel unaffordable for middle class families. They had no option but to take the land route.

The only land border crossing open at that time was the one between Wagah (near Lahore) in Pakistan and Atari (near Amritsar) in India. Therefore, a family wanting to travel between Karachi on the one side and Bombay, Ahmedabad, Hyderabad (Deccan), Lucknow or Patna on the other had to undertake a really, really long and tough journey. They would travel over a 1000 km by train from Karachi all the way north to Lahore, cross over into India and then travel another 1500 km or more before reaching their destination. Taking into account the time involved in crossing the border and waiting for onward trains, the entire journey took more than three days each way! Additionally, the fact that most people undertook the journey to India during the summer vacations made it even more gruelling. It was only their yearning for their parents and other near and dear ones that gave people the strength and fortitude to undertake such a journey year after year.

This problem relating to a circuitous and time-consuming route had not existed till 1965 as another Indo-Pak border crossing had been available. This was the Khokhrapar-Munabao checkpoint at the Sindh-Rajasthan border. The Sindh Mail ran from Karachi to Ahmedabad via this border, passing through cities like Hyderabad and Mirpur Khas in Pakistan, and Jodhpur in India. The journey from Karachi to India used to be much shorter. However, this link was destroyed during the 1965 Indo-Pak War, and although Indian troops rebuilt it when they captured Khokhrapar in the 1971 War, the route was not re-opened on account of the unwillingness of the Pakistani authorities.

Why were the Pakistanis unwilling to reopen the Khokhrapar-Munabao route? No doubt, they had security concerns. Sindh was their soft underbelly; they felt extremely vulnerable there and wanted to keep the border very tightly controlled.

However, another reason for their obduracy was the objection from the powerful Punjabi lobby in Lahore which had thriving businesses operating at the Wagah-Atari checkpoint. Several thousand persons crossed the Wagah-Atari border every week, and goods also moved between the two countries through this route. Naturally, a large number of service-providers were required, for example custom-clearing houses, transport agencies, hotels, restaurants and souvenir shops. They all had a roaring business on this account. Even porters made a tidy sum from travellers. If the *Muhajirs* from Karachi or elsewhere in Sindh could take the Khokhrapar-Munabao route, all such businesses in Lahore stood to lose their monopoly and thereby suffer considerable losses.

Thus, although we repeatedly approached the Pakistan Government to reopen the Kokhrapar-Munabao rail route, they would just not do so. The net result was that the common man in the *Muhajir* community continued to suffer, but the authorities in Islamabad were not bothered about this at all. This was a huge contrast to the sympathetic and helpful attitude of the Indian side on matters concerning visas, inter-country travel and related issues.

I recall a Pakistani journalist telling Consul General Parthasarathy that his popularity in Karachi was so high that were he to contest an election there, he would win hands down! Coming from a *Muhajir*, the comment was a reflection of how this community felt let down by their own government.

It may be mentioned here that the *Muhajirs* had many grievances that had been festering for a long time. In the beginning of Pakistan's history, these migrants had better educational qualifications and were consequently able to play a dominant role in bureaucracy as well in educational institutions. However, when President Ayub Khan introduced the quota system, the provinces of Pakistan were given representation in the bureaucracy and in practically every field according to the percentage of their population. This arrangement provided for a very small share for the urban areas of Sindh, such as Karachi, Hyderabad and the other cities where the *Muhajirs* lived. At the same time, it was heavily tilted in favour of the Punjabis,

Pashtuns and Sindhis. The quota system was progressively enlarged to include more institutions.

The share of the *Muhajirs* in government positions kept going down progressively, and soon, they began to find it more difficult to get admission in institutions for higher learning. Many Muslims from all over India had migrated to Pakistan thinking that they were going to the 'Land of the Pure', and one that was full of opportunities. However, they were slowly disillusioned. Naturally, this bred discontent and unhappiness that led to the creation of the *Muhajir Qaumi Movement* (MQM) as a political party in March 1984. The huge rallies of the MQM were a portent that it was going to play an important role not just in Karachi, but in national level politics as well.

As part of its agenda to address the problems of *Muhajirs*, the MQM started exerting pressure on Islamabad to reopen the Khokhrapar-Munabao crossing, and these efforts succeeded in 2006 when the Thar Express started to run between Karachi and Jodhpur. This shortened the travel time to India considerably and it is thus no longer necessary for those wanting to travel by train from Karachi to destinations in India to go via the Lahore-Amritsar border.

It had taken more than four decades to reopen this route after it was closed during the 1965 Indo-Pakistan War.

Flames of the Chinar

XVII

I once asked a Pakistani diplomat why they made it so difficult for Indian applicants to get visas. After all, they just wanted to visit their close relatives—sons, daughters, brothers, sisters, etc. What was wrong with that?

I got a bizarre reply: "Because these applicants will stay back in Pakistan and will not go back to India as economic conditions are better here." What a joke, I thought to myself!

I pointed out that the unemployment rate and inflation were both much higher in Pakistan and that India was a much bigger economy with many more employment opportunities. I asked teasingly, "In any case, wasn't Pakistan established so that the Muslims of the Indian sub-continent could live in a separate homeland? Why object if some Muslims from India want to come and live here?"

He had no answer to my query. Somewhat rattled and irritated, he said rather brusquely "Don't expect anything from us if you don't give us Kashmir".

There is no denying the fact that for the Pakistanis, Jammu and Kashmir is an obsession they cannot let go of, and because of which they continue to unleash violence and mayhem over there whenever they can. They are clearly in violation of the Simla Agreement signed after the 1971 War which states that *the two countries are resolved to settle their differences by peaceful means through bilateral negotiations or by any other peaceful means mutually agreed upon between them. Pending the final settlement of any of the problems between the two countries, neither side shall unilaterally alter the situation, and both shall prevent the organization, assistance or encouragement of any acts detrimental to the maintenance of peace and harmonious relations.*

Instead, the Pakistanis keep harping that India has failed to carry out the plebiscite in terms of the 1948 UN Security Council Resolution adopted on 21 April 1948. Therefore, in our discussions we have categorically told them that it is necessary to look at the provisions of the resolution to understand how it is Pakistan, and not India which is really at fault.

Operative Para 1 of the Resolution of 21 April 1948 states the following:

1) *The Government of Pakistan should undertake to use its best endeavours:*

   (a) *To secure the withdrawal from the State of Jammu and Kashmir of tribesmen and Pakistani Nationals not normally resident therein, who have entered the State for the purposes of fighting and to prevent any intrusion into the State of such elements and any furnishing of material aid to those fighting in the State.*

   (b) *To make known to all concerned that the measures indicated in this and the following paragraphs provide full freedom to all subjects of the State, regardless of creed, caste*

> *or party, to express their views and to vote on the question*
> *of the accession of the State, and that therefore they should*
> *cooperate in the maintenance of peace and order.*

Para 2(a) lays down the following:

2)   The Government of India should:

> *(a) When it is established to the satisfaction of the*
> *Commission set up in accordance with the Council's*
> *resolution of 20 January that the tribesmen are*
> *withdrawing and that arrangements for the cessation of*
> *the fighting have become effective, put into operation in*
> *consultation with the Commission, a plan for*
> *withdrawing their own forces from Jammu and Kashmir*
> *and reducing them progressively to the minimum*
> *strength required for the support of civil power in the*
> *maintenance of law and order.*

Once the above mentioned pre-conditions were met, the arrangements for the plebiscite were to be made. However, Pakistan did not comply with the requirements of Para 1 of the Resolution as it did not do anything to ensure the withdrawal of the tribesmen and its nationals from Jammu and Kashmir. Due to this, the remainder of the resolution could not be implemented and became null and void.

The UN Commission for India and Pakistan Resolution dated 13 August 1948 is even more categorical in this respect as it refers to the presence of Pakistani troops constituting a material change in the situation.

Part II A states the following relating to the responsibility of Pakistan:

1) *As the presence of troops of Pakistan in the territory of the State of Jammu and Kashmir constitutes a material change in the situation since it was represented by the Government of Pakistan before the Security Council, the Government of Pakistan agrees to withdraw its troops from that state.*

2) *The Government of Pakistan will use its best endeavour to secure the withdrawal from the State of Jammu and Kashmir of tribesmen and Pakistani nationals not normally resident therein who have entered the State for the purpose of fighting.*

3) *Pending a final solution, the territory evacuated by the Pakistani troops will be administered by the local authorities under the surveillance of the Commission.*

Part II B of the Resolution then states what the ensuing responsibility of India will be:

1) *When the Commission shall have notified the Government of India that the tribesmen and Pakistani nationals referred to in Part II, A, 2, hereof have withdrawn, thereby terminating the situation which was represented by the Government of India to the Security Council as having occasioned the presence of Indian forces in the State of Jammu and Kashmir, and further that the Pakistani troops are being withdrawn from the State of Jammu and Kashmir, the Government of India agrees to begin to withdraw the bulk of its forces from that State in stages to be agreed upon with the Commission.*

2) *Pending the acceptance of the conditions for a final settlement of the situation in the State of Jammu and Kashmir, the Indian Government will maintain within the lines existing at the moment of the cease-fire the minimum strength of its forces which in agreement with the Commission are considered necessary to assist local authorities in the observance of law and order. The Commission will have observers stationed where it deems necessary.*

3) *The Government of India will undertake to ensure that the Government of the State of Jammu and Kashmir will take all measures within its powers to make it publicly known that peace, law and order will be safeguarded and that all human political rights will be granted.*

4) *Upon signature, the full text of the truce agreement or a communique containing the principles thereof as agreed upon between the two Governments and the Commission, will be made public.*

Part III then goes on to say the following:

The Government of India and the Government of Pakistan reaffirm their wish that the future status of the State of Jammu and Kashmir shall be determined in accordance with the will of the people and to that end, upon acceptance of the truce agreement, both Governments agree to enter into consultations with the Commission to determine fair and equitable conditions whereby such free expression will be assured.

Pakistan's shrill argument that India was responsible for the non-implementation of the UN resolutions on Jammu and

Kashmir does not have a leg to stand on. The fact remains that Pakistan itself did not execute its own responsibilities laid down in Part II A for withdrawing its troops from Jammu and Kashmir and securing the withdrawal of its own nationals and tribesmen that had infiltrated into the State. Since this pre-condition was not fulfilled by it, the remainder of this resolution was un-implementable and hence automatically became null and void.

During the years that have elapsed since these UN Resolutions were adopted, Pakistan has continued to change the demographic structure of the part of Jammu and Kashmir it occupies by helping the Punjabis and Pathans to settle down there. It has also changed the geography of the State by ceding a large tract of land to China. The UN Resolutions related to a situation which existed in 1948, and which has been materially altered by a series of unending actions by Pakistan.

The elephant and ......

XVIII

The UN Resolutions on Jammu and Kashmir are dead and buried. Although the Pakistanis themselves are responsible for this, they somehow remain blind-sighted to this fact. The Pakistani mindset does not change in the least bit, and it was not a wee bit surprising when the current Pakistan Ambassador Abdul Basit said in an interview in May 2015 that 'The Kashmir dispute is the mother of all problems'.

The Pakistanis continue to bring Kashmir into every discussion relating to the bilateral relationship – this is something that never changes. According to them, restrictions on trade, visas, travel and cultural exchanges could be eased and the relationship normalised only after the Kashmir issue gets resolved. They continue to harp on the theme that Kashmir is Pakistan's jugular vein, and their public posturing creates the impression that the only acceptable solution would be for India to hand over the whole of Jammu and Kashmir to them.

On its part, India too claims that whole of Jammu and Kashmir belongs to it, and that Pakistan must vacate the part which is occupied by it. India also asserts that Pakistan illegally ceded 5180 square kilometres of territory in Jammu and Kashmir to China in 1963.

Many Indians feel that after our decisive victory in the 1971 War, we should have settled the Kashmir dispute with finality, and that those in charge of the negotiations on our side did not do so, and thereby failed the nation.

Even if the dispute had been settled in this manner, would the Pakistanis have lived peacefully with us as good neighbours? Most certainly not; they would have done precisely what they have always been doing – sending infiltrators to create as much mayhem as possible and abetting separatism in Jammu and Kashmir. They would have always done whatever possible to keep the Kashmir issue on the front burner. It is completely unlikely that they would have undergone a change of heart if a settlement had been forced on them after the 1971 war. A settlement they did not subscribe to from their hearts would not have been worth the parchment on which it was written.

In other words, although a conclusive settlement of the Kashmir dispute after our victory in the 1971 war may have been preferable to an agreement which merely stipulates that the two countries have agreed to settle all disputes bilaterally, it appears unlikely that it would have ended the problem. Pakistan would have continued to covet Kashmir; it would not have given up its policy of fomenting trouble not just in Kashmir, but wherever possible in India.

Unfortunately, our diplomats have to pay a heavy price for Pakistan's hostility arising from its Kashmir policy; they often undergo a harrowing time, as I experienced first-hand during my posting in Karachi.

However, before saying anything about my experience, let me recount some of the more serious incidents that took place around that time.

On February 3, 1984, Ravindra Mhatre, the Assistant High Commissioner of India in Birmingham was kidnapped by the Jammu and Kashmir Liberation Front (JKLF), an organisation sponsored and funded by the Pakistan Government. The kidnappers demanded a ransom as well as the release of some Kashmiri terrorists including Maqbool Butt, who was facing a death sentence in India for killing a policeman in Jammu and Kashmir. Mhatre's body was found two days later. The Indian Government reacted swiftly and Maqbool Butt was hanged on February 11, 1984.

This led to an attack on our Consulate building in Karachi by a stone-throwing group of protesters. Consul General G. Parthasarathy's car was attacked as it was about to enter the Consulate gate, and its windshield was smashed by a mob. Fortunately, the Consul General escaped unhurt, but one shudders at the thought of what could have happened.

A few nights later, I received a telephone call. The caller merely said "Mr. Dayal, you will be killed tonight after midnight at your residence." Before I could say anything, the caller repeated the message and hung up.

We alerted the Pakistani authorities, who provided me with police protection. Nothing untoward happened, but given the background of the events of the previous weeks, it was a rather uneasy period in my diplomatic career.

Later I heard that some of my other colleagues were also subjected to threats. Clearly, the entire affair was being masterminded by the Pakistani authorities to unsettle us. Had they wanted, they could have easily arrested the persons who attacked the Consul General's car. They could have also traced the number from which the telephonic threat to me had been made. However, they did nothing of the sort.

Could the Pakistani authorities have prevented the attack on our Consulate? They could have certainly done so. Although the Consulate was provided with police protection by them, the attackers lay in ambush quite close to where the policemen stood and came running to attack when they saw the Consul General's car approaching. The police personnel did not move from their positions and looked on as mere spectators when the Consul General's car was attacked! No doubt, the attack was carried out with the full knowledge and approval of Pakistani authorities.

Again, couldn't the authorities have traced the caller who made the telephonic threat to me? No doubt they could have done so, as we knew that they were tapping all our phones. We had this unavoidable feeling that they were behind the whole sordid chapter.

Anyone who has followed Indo-Pak relations would not entertain much hope about the foreseeable future. Without doubt, the single biggest factor that has bedevilled the relationship, and which will continue to do so, is the Kashmir problem, as it is an obsession for Pakistan.

I feel compelled to tell a story here.

An essay contest was organised for students from the Diplomatic Academies of different countries. The topic for the essay was the elephant, and the students were asked to write on any aspect that they wanted. The British student wrote on 'The elephant and the British Empire', the American student wrote on 'The elephant as a business proposition', the Indian wrote on 'The elephant as an endangered species', while the French wrote on 'The love life of the elephant'.

What did the Pakistani student write on? He wrote on 'The elephant and the Kashmir problem'.

Helping hands

XIX

Not only were all our telephones bugged, the Pakistani counter intelligence ensured that we were tailed and kept under surveillance at all times.

A large number of the diplomats posted at the Pakistan Embassy in Delhi were ISI operatives, and therefore the Pakistan authorities presumed (quite wrongly) that the majority of Indian diplomats posted in Pakistan were also agents of RAW. This is why they kept us under a very close watch.

Throughout my posting in Pakistan, I was tailed by two persons whose faces are etched in my memory as I saw them following me all the time every single day on their motorbike. One of them was a tall, fair man with a moustache, while the other was shorter, darker and bearded. One of them would be driving, while the other would be riding pillion. I could not go anywhere without being followed by them.

Mary had a little lamb,

His fleece was white as snow,

And everywhere that Mary went,

The lamb was sure to go.

Of course, these two persons were not really lambs – they were more like fearsome wolves! If I went into a shop, they would also come in and stand quite close to me. If I went to a restaurant, they would come inside to see who I was meeting there. I don't think I've ever been subjected to such intrusive surveillance in any of my other postings.

If I went to anyone's house, they would stand outside the gate. Later, they would go inside the house to enquire why I had come there. In some instances, the occupants of the house were even asked to come to the police station to be grilled about their contacts with me! Naturally, many people preferred to keep away from such hassles, and this meant a sudden cooling off in their relations with us. I lost many friends in this manner.

One night, when I was returning from a dinner, my car had a flat tyre. The two persons who were tailing me also stopped, though at a distance.

I had never changed a tyre in my life, and was at a loss about what I should do. I took out the jack and the tool kit from the boot of the car, and was trying to figure out how to go about the business of changing the tyre.

Suddenly, I had a brainwave. Such brainwaves come rarely, but that night I was quite lucky.

I walked up to where the two gentlemen were standing. They became uneasy to see me approaching them.

Very coolly, I told them to come and change my tyre.

They seemed to ignore what I was telling them.

I told them in a very matter-of-fact way that I could not go back home because of the flat tyre, and that they too would not be able to go to their homes as long as I did not move from this spot. We would all be just stranded here unless they helped me to change the tyre.

I was able to get my point across, and they walked over to my car and changed the tyre. Once this was done, we drove towards my house and having seen me go in, they proceeded to their own.

Surprisingly, they became a bit friendlier and less intimidating after this incident. The ice had been broken, and a hint of cordiality came into our relationship. I would smile when I saw them, and they would smile back. Of course, they had to do their job, but the earlier phase when we did not even acknowledge one another was a thing of the past. It had gone with a gust of wind from a burst tyre!

Not only were we (Indian diplomats) followed by counter-intelligence persons all the time, our movements were also severely curtailed. We were not allowed to leave the city limits of Karachi without prior permission, and such permission was rarely accorded. On the other hand, Pakistani diplomats in India merely had to intimate the External Affairs Ministry that they were going out of Delhi. This showed that we were not following the principle of reciprocity, which we should have been doing.

During my career I realised that many countries are not as generous when it comes to according diplomatic and consular privileges as we are in India. In other words, very often the privileges we accord to foreign diplomats are much more than the corresponding privileges Indian diplomats get abroad.

The Pakistan authorities claimed that they needed to ensure our security before allowing us to go out of Karachi, but this was not the real reason. They were afraid that we would undertake outstation trips to areas which were simmering with discontent. They also feared that we would utilize the opportunity provided by such trips to meet separatist groups; after all, Pakistani diplomats in India regularly meet Kashmiri separatist elements.

Separatism was rife not only in the North West Frontier Province of Pakistan, but also in Sindh and Baluchistan, the two provinces which were under the jurisdiction of our Consulate in Karachi.

The Jeay Sindh movement had been started in 1972 in Sindh by the veteran leader GM Syed with the intention to secede from Pakistan and form Sindhudesh. Syed was inspired by the creation of Bangladesh.

The Jeay Sindh movement espoused the view that Sindhis were being disenfranchised and not being given the rights and privileges that had been originally promised to them when a federal structure was established in Pakistan.

Earlier in his political career, GM Syed had worked hard for the creation of Pakistan, and had in fact, lobbied to have the bill for the creation of Pakistan passed in the Sindh Assembly. However, as time went by he became disenchanted and disowned the idea of Pakistan as he felt that the principles of federalism were being betrayed, as also because of the growing domination of Punjabis at the expense of other ethnic groups.

Once Bangladesh was formed, it only served to strengthen his belief that the idea of Pakistani nationhood was unsustainable. He completely disavowed the idea of Pakistan which he had at one time himself espoused.

GM Syed was arrested time and again, but the movement he had started kept gaining momentum. However, the Pakistan army brutally cracked down on Sindhi separatists, killing hundreds of them and arresting thousands of others.

While the Pakistan Government blamed India for the rise of Sindhi separatism, Syed himself lamented the fact that India had done nothing at all to help them. He reportedly told his confidantes that if India were to help the separatist movement in Sindh, they would be able to break away from Pakistan as Bangladesh had done.

Syed died in April 1995. However, Sindhi separatism has far from died down and on 23 March 2014, the Sindh Freedom march in Karachi was attended by more than five million persons.[13] Such separatist outpourings continue to be witnessed in various parts of Sindh from time to time.

In fact, Sindhi separatism has assumed a more menacing dimension after the formation of the Sindhudesh Liberation Army with the avowed aim of creating a separate Sindhudesh. As would be expected, the Pakistan Government has accused India of supporting the Sindhudesh Liberation Army while trying to distract attention from the fact that its own policies have bred discontent among the Sindhis.

Even more worrisome for Pakistan has been Baloch separatism which has assumed dangerously militant dimensions from time to time, and which the Pakistan army has tried to put down ruthlessly. Although Balochistan is the largest of the provinces of Pakistan and covers 44% of the area, it is the least populated with only 5% of the population. It is also the least economically developed with the vast majority of the population lacking even basic amenities.

Baloch separatism is much more deep rooted in history. Balochistan consisted of four princely states under the British Raj — Kalat, Makran, Las Bela and Kharan. In 1947, the Khan of Kalat, the ruler of the largest of these princely states chose independence, which was an option given to all the 535 princely states. The other Balochi chiefs also expressed their preference for a separate identity. However, Pakistan sent in its army which forced the Khan of Kalat to give up his independence. The Khan signed the instrument of accession on 27 March 1948, over seven months after the formation of Pakistan.

Even after the accession of Kalat to Pakistan, Baloch separatism has continued to rear its menacing head from time to time. Major conflicts between Baloch separatists and the Pakistan army took place in 1948, 1958-59, 1963-69 and 1973-77. A large number of Balochi guerrilla fighters and civilians have been killed in the operations conducted by the Pakistan army. It is estimated that between 2003 and 2012, over 8000 Balochis disappeared after they were abducted by Pakistani security forces.[14]

The Pakistani media was subjected to strict censorship, and reports about the ongoing human rights violations in Sindh and Balochistan were not allowed to appear. However we would come to know what was going on through our local Pakistani friends. Sometimes there would be demonstrations in Karachi to protest over some particular incident, and word would be out about whatever had happened. Despite the unrelenting efforts of the military junta to muzzle the press, the people in Pakistan as well as elsewhere were fully aware of the seriousness of the situation in these two provinces.

XX

Although the Pakistani authorities did not normally give us permission to go to other cities in our Consular jurisdiction, sometimes situations arose when they had no option but to allow us. One such opportunity arose in 1984 when the Indian Foreign Secretary MK Rasgotra, who was on an official visit to Islamabad expressed a desire to visit Mohenjodaro. Consul General Parthasarathy sent me on protocol and liaison duty for this visit.

Mohenjodaro is a highly important archaeological site in Sindh. Built around 2600 BC, it was one of the largest settlements of the Indus Valley Civilisation, and one of the world's earliest urban settlements. A contemporary of ancient Egypt and Mesopotamia, Mohenjodaro is a UNESCO Word Heritage site. I was extremely excited at this opportunity to visit a place which has such an exalted status in Indian history! Mohenjodaro is situated on the west bank of the river Indus in Larkana district of Sindh, which is home to the Bhutto family.

My visit to Larkana was a real eye opener for me, as it showed me how backward the hinterland of Sindh was. Although Larkana is one of the bigger cities of this province, its infrastructure was absolutely pathetic. I took a plane from Karachi and landed at Larkana airport where I got the first taste of things.

The airport itself was highly disorganised and ill managed. I wanted to use the washroom there before proceeding to Mohenjodaro. I can say with absolute certainty that it was the dirtiest washroom I had ever seen at any airport in the world. Even the toilets at Indian railway stations are much better kept than the one I saw at Larkana Airport. It was a far cry from the toilets at airports in India.

The roads were full of potholes, garbage was lying all around the city and dirty, unkempt children were playing all around in what was supposed to be the city centre. The neglect and apathy of the administration was writ large. Was this because it was Bhutto's city? Were the people of Larkana being punished because they had supported Bhutto when he was alive? Or, were they marginalised because they had resisted Martial Law, which was imposed and maintained by the Punjabi-dominated army of Pakistan?

I understand that in later years, particularly during the period when Benazir Bhutto was Prime Minister, Larkana was given a tremendous facelift. However, when I visited it in 1984, it was still in quite a pathetic state.

I can never forget a discussion with some of my Pakistani friends about the disparities that existed in Pakistan. One said that Islamabad was so beautifully maintained, whereupon someone else rather cynically remarked that Islamabad was one hundred miles from Pakistan. As I saw the pathetic conditions in Larkana, I could not help but agree with him. The capital city of Pakistan is indeed far removed from much of the hinterland.

Before proceeding to Mohenjodaro, I went to Zulfiqar Ali Bhutto's mausoleum in Garhi Khuda Bakhsh village in

Larkana. It was deserted with only a solitary caretaker there. In later years, during Benazir Bhutto's rule, it became the venue for numerous events held in the memory of her late father. A few decades later, such events were also held in her own memory as she too lies buried there after her tragic assassination in December 2007.

I was given accommodation in the government-run guest house in Mohenjodaro, which was nothing more than a modest shack. It had a creaky bed and an apology of a bathroom. There was a window-air conditioner which was so noisy that it was better left turned off. Tragically, there was no alternative to this guest house as Mohenjodaro had no hotels whatsoever.

I was amazed that the Pakistani authorities had done nothing to develop the tourism prospects of such a remarkable historical site. The ruins of Mohenjodaro were reasonably well maintained as it was a UNESCO Heritage site, but I could not spot any tourists. The Indian Foreign Secretary and his delegation were the only ones visiting Mohenjodaro, which was rather surprising given the archaeological importance of the place.

Why had the Pakistan Government done nothing whatsoever to encourage tourists to visit Mohenjodaro? Why were no hotels built there? No doubt this was because Mohenjodaro was a part of Pakistan's pre-Islamic history which was not something that its present rulers were particularly interested in exalting. It is possible that they wanted to restrict the flow of international traffic to Larkana due to the attention this would inevitably draw to the Bhutto family, something which Pakistan's military rulers at that time were loath to let happen.

Nonetheless, it was a real treat as far as I was concerned to be able to visit this jewel of the Indus Valley civilisation. Mohenjodaro was spread over an area of around 300 hectares, and it is estimated that the city had once been home to around 40,000 people, making it one of the largest urban settlements of the third millennium BC. I was amazed how such a planned city had been built over four and a half thousand years ago! The buildings along rectilinear streets were made from bricks, and the meticulously planned drainage system was evidence of a high standard of public works. Among the ruins I saw were those of the great granary, a market place, public baths, houses for the rich as well as the less well-off and two large assembly halls.

While going around the ruins of this ancient city, I reflected how, if given the chance tourists from India would have flocked to Mohenjodaro. I cannot help but contrast this with the apathy among Pakistanis towards this archaeological marvel. I spoke to several people in Karachi about my visit to Mohenjodaro, and I was surprised that none of them had ever visited it, nor had any plans to do so!

This place, which was on the list of UNESCO'S heritage sites was not on the itinerary of Pakistani tourists! How sad, I thought to myself!

✦ ✦ ✦

XXI

The Indian cricket team's tours in 1982-83 and 1984, respectively, also provided us some rare and much-needed opportunities to visit other cities in Pakistan. The visits of our team as well as the huge media party accompanying it necessitated liaison work with the local authorities. The Pakistani authorities could not deny us permission to visit cities outside Karachi by dishing out the usual excuse about their concern about our security, as the matches themselves could not have been held if security was inadequate.

Moreover, in the event of the Pakistan authorities not granting us permission to go to the matches with the team, the large number of Indian journalists covering the cricket series would have definitely mentioned this in their despatches, which would have attracted adverse attention. Therefore, willy-nilly the Pakistan Foreign Office had to give us permission to accompany the team. Looking back, these visits were not merely enjoyable on account of the cricket, but also very educative.

During the 1982-83 tour by the Indian cricket team, there was a one-day match in Multan, and on this occasion I accompanied Consul General Parthasarathy to this historic city. Regarded as the city of Sufi saints, Multan is dotted with a large number of their shrines and ornate tombs. I visited the two most famous mausoleums of Sheikh Baha-ud-Din Zakariya and Shah Rukn-e-Alam whose beautiful domes dominate the skyline.

Multan is said to have derived its name from the Sanskrit name *Mulasthana* meaning Sun Temple. I was shown some ruins near the Multan High Court, which are said to be those of the Sun Temple, but there is no agreement among scholars in this regard because the temple was destroyed long ago. Besides, so many temples had been destroyed in Multan during the Muslim rule lasting more than a thousand years, that the ruins shown to me could have been those of any such temple.

The Sun Temple in Multan is said to have been built by Lord Krishna's son Samba. It is mentioned by the Greek Admiral Scylax who is said to have visited the area in 515 BC. The Chinese traveller Huien Tsang also visited the temple in 640 AD and described the statue of the sun god made of gold with eyes made of red rubies. When the Arab invader Muhammad bin Qasim conquered Multan in the 8th Century AD, he looted the temple but did not destroy the statue, though historical accounts suggest that he hung a piece of cow flesh over its neck to mock it. The temple was finally destroyed by Mahmud of Ghazni in 1026 AD and has never been rebuilt since.

I also visited the Prahladpuri temple. According to mythology, the original temple was built by Prahlad in honour of the half-man half-lion god Narasimha, who is believed to be an incarnation of Lord Vishnu. The temple was repeatedly destroyed by the Muslims and rebuilt by the Hindus of Multan. It was a modest temple when I went there in December 1982. I learnt that there were only a handful of devotees who went there daily. Of course, this was due to the fact that almost all the Hindus of Multan had migrated to India!

The Prahladpuri temple was completely destroyed by a violent Muslim mob in 1992 [15]. This was just ten years after I had visited it. I felt sad when I learnt about its destruction.

The cricket match was held at the famous Ibn-e-Qasim Bagh Stadium, inside the Multan Fort. Surrounded by historical buildings, it was a beautiful setting. I sat next to the Deputy Commissioner of Multan, a learned gentleman, who gave me a very informative background briefing on the city. He also told me that according to popular local belief, Alexander conquered Multan, but during the fighting, he was injured by an arrow which caused a slow deterioration in his health and ultimately led to his death.

During the 1984 tour by the Indian team, I got the opportunity to visit Quetta where a one-day match was held. Situated at a height of almost 1700 metres, Quetta is near the Bolan-pass route between Central and South Asia. It has numerous fruit orchards, due to which it is called the Fruit Garden of Pakistan. Most of the old city had been destroyed in the earthquake of 1935, but despite this, Quetta retains a distinctly historical character.

Even though Quetta is very important politically, being the capital of Baluchistan province, it appeared to be quite underdeveloped. Many of the roads were not tarred. Quite a few of the buildings seemed to have seen better days, reflecting a state of general apathy and neglect. It is hardly surprising that a separatist insurgency has been active there for several decades, almost since the very beginning of Pakistan's history.

One major problem I encountered on these rare trips outside Karachi was the complete absence of vegetarian items on the menus of the restaurants in the hotels I stayed in – a testimony to the fact that Pakistanis are compulsive meat eaters. While some arrangements must surely have been made for the vegetarians in our cricket team, I had to manage with bread and salad at almost every meal in my hotel.

While on this subject, let me mention that whenever I was invited to the homes of my Pakistani friends in Karachi, I would inform them in advance that I was a vegetarian. They would subject me to endless leg-pulling and ask me as to why I ate only leaves and grass. Thankfully, it was their *begums* (wives) who ruled over the kitchens, and the delicious vegetarian food which I got to savour at their homes was surely ambrosia – food fit for the gods!

Put paid to all that talk.....

XXII

Cricket is an important ingredient of the Indo-Pakistan relationship. I witnessed two tours by the Indian team during my stay in Karachi – during 1982-83 and in 1984, respectively.

When the Indian team toured Pakistan in 1982-83, I discovered that my boss G. Parthasarathy, the Indian Consul General was a good cricketer himself, and that even more importantly, he was a firm believer in Indo-Pak cricket diplomacy. Partha would go out of his way to ensure the well-being of our cricket team as he knew that the tour of Pakistan could be very stressful. Whenever the team members played in Karachi, they would be invited to his residence practically every evening for beer and *dosas*; this combination, which was a favourite of many of the team members, was not available in such plenty anywhere else except in Partha's house.

The whole idea of these cricket tours was to promote friendship between the Indians and the Pakistanis, but it is debatable that this objective was being actually realised. The eminent Indian sports writer and commentator KR Wadhwaney evaluated the matter quite correctly in his book *Indian Cricket Controversies*:

It is a total misnomer that the series between India and Pakistan brings (the) players and peoples of the two countries together. Cricket between India and Pakistan is no longer a sport to enjoy and recreate, but it is a war game, which promotes violence and accusations of cheating through umpires. [16]

A historical perspective of India-Pakistan cricket is necessary here. India toured Pakistan in 1952-53, and Pakistan paid a return visit in 1954-55. Pakistan again visited India in 1960-61. No cricket tours were exchanged between 1961 and 1978 due to the Indo-Pak wars of 1965 and 1971, respectively. The resumption of cricketing ties took place in 1978 when Bishen Singh Bedi led the Indian team to Pakistan. This was followed by a return visit to India by the Pakistan team led by Asif Iqbal in 1979-80. Both the series were won by the home teams. Thus, the stage was set for the 1982-83 series which I was privileged to watch first-hand.

The two teams were rather evenly matched, but what tilted the results completely in favour of the Pakistanis was the biased umpiring. Atrocious umpiring decisions favouring the home team ensured that the cricket matches were reduced to a farce. Of course, controversies surrounding biased umpiring in Pakistan have marred not just the tours of the Indian team but those by other teams too. The English cricketer Ian Botham reportedly said: *You wouldn't see such decisions in village cricket, leave alone test cricket.*[17]

In due course, such controversies became a driving force for the introduction of neutral umpires in international cricket.

That the Pakistan umpires would come down heavily against the visiting Indian team was not unexpected, if past experience was to be a guide. During the earlier tour in 1978, many umpiring incidents had marred the game, and the Indian team had been furious over the double standards of Pakistani umpiring. For example, they were upset that Umpire Shakoor Rana had warned India's Mohinder Amarnath for running on the pitch when he had no such problems with the Pakistani bowlers doing the same.

Even more telling is this quote from Shashi Tharoor and Shahrayar Khan's book *Shadows Across the Playing Field*:

In recalling events when he assumed Pakistan's captaincy, Imran Khan revealed his shock when umpires appointed for the test called on him and asked him for special instructions, if any![18]

Recalling his 1982-83 tour of Pakistan, the Indian cricketer Ravi Shastri said: *Imran and Sarfraz would make the ball swing, and then there were those two umpires Khizer Hayat and Shakoor Rana. It was like playing a four-pronged pace attack.*[19]

Six test matches were played in the 1982-83 series of which Pakistan won three while the other three were drawn. In addition, 4 one-day matches were played, of which Pakistan won three. After their resounding success in this bilateral series, Pakistani newspapers began harping on the theme that their team was far superior to the Indian team.

This blowing-their-own-trumpet sort of routine went on and on till something happened to suddenly prick their balloon. In July 1983, India won the *Cricket World Cup* held in England! Interestingly, India defeated the West Indies, who had soundly thrashed Pakistan in the semi-finals!

Before the final, many of my Pakistani friends, some of whom were sports journalists had told me rather patronisingly that getting to the final itself was a great achievement for the Indian team. It was apparent that none of them expected India to beat West Indies.

I cannot forget the sense of disbelief that prevailed all over Pakistan after India won the final. Neither can I forget the eerie silence that descended over Karachi that evening as realisation set in that Indians were now the world champions in a sport which was the greatest passion for Pakistanis. It was as if Pakistan had gone into mourning!

Within a few months, however, the Pakistani media had recovered its bravado and was waxing eloquent on the theme that the Indian victory over the mighty West Indies in the World Cup was proof that cricket was a game of glorious uncertainties. They were confident that the Pakistani team would establish its superiority over India sooner or later.

Though the Indian team's tour to Pakistan in 1984 was abruptly cut short due to Mrs. Gandhi's assassination, an opportunity soon presented itself to the Pakistanis when the World Championship of Cricket was held in Australia in Feb-March 1985. Besides the hosts Australia, it was contested by England, New Zealand, West Indies, Sri Lanka, India and Pakistan.

Against all odds, India and Pakistan reached the finals of this championship by outclassing Australia as well as such formidable teams as the West Indies, England and New

Zealand. The stage was now set for an epic clash between the two teams from the sub-continent, and it took place on 12 March 1985.

In both countries, the people were glued to their television sets, but as things unfolded, India completely routed Pakistan, winning by eight wickets. The scores were: Pakistan 176 for 9 wickets, India 177 for 2 wickets. To rub salt in the wounds of the Pakistanis, the winning team was adjudged by Wisden (the Bible of cricket) as 'India's team of the century'! Ravi Shastri won the award for the 'Champion of Champions' and walked away with the coveted prize—an Audi.

Once again, Pakistan went into mourning.

Less than two weeks later, India and Pakistan again played on 22 March at the 4- nation *Rothman's Cup* held in Sharjah. India batted first and was dismissed for a paltry total of 125 runs. This score was extremely low by any standards, and the Pakistanis were confident that there was no way they could lose this game. But they lost yet again as their team collapsed for a mere 87 runs! To make matters even more unpalatable for the Pakistanis, the Indian team went on to win the final against Australia and clinch the *Rothman's Cup* too!

My stay in Pakistan thus saw the highs and lows in the cricketing rivalry between the two sides. Pakistan was unbeatable at home with their umpires around to help out, but they capitulated in three major international tournaments in quick succession while India romped home as champions. The

Indian team bagged the *Cricket World Cup* in England (1983), the *World Championship of Cricket* in Australia (Feb-March 1985) and the *Rothman's Cup* in Sharjah (March 1985). As regards all the bragging in the Pakistani media about how their team was superior, the Indian team had authoritatively put paid to all that!

A Murree with your curree!

XXIII

Without doubt, cricket ignites very strong passions in our two nations. A cricket match between India and Pakistan is not a mere sporting event, but a highly loaded and charged affair due to the history of the bitter and hostile political relationship. Sadly, I found that many Pakistanis viewed these cricket matches not as between two national teams, but between Muslims and Hindus.

Nothing brings out this fact more clearly than an incident that remains in my mind. From my childhood, I had heard of Abdul Hafeez Kardar, who had been Pakistan's first ever captain from 1952-58. He had also been the President of the Pakistan Cricket Board from 1972-77. Thus, he was an influential figure in Pakistan cricket, reflecting the views of the establishment quite clearly. When I met him during the Indian team's tour in 1982, he came across as a rather arrogant and opinionated person.

During the 1987 tour of India by the Pakistani team, the commentary team of Pakistan TV included Kardar. When Pakistan achieved a close victory in the Bangalore Test, Kardar could not control his emotions and shouted hysterically on TV: *We have beaten the Hindus in their own land, we have conquered the Hindus.*[20]

This distasteful comment was a reflection on how Kardar as also many of his countrymen looked at these cricket matches between our two countries. While making such an obnoxious comment, Kardar seemed to have overlooked the fact that the Indian team which lost in the above mentioned Bangalore test was a multi-religious team reflecting the secular nature of India. It included Mohammad Azharuddin, Roger Binny and Maninder Singh, none of whom were Hindus.

For the benefit of the people in Pakistan who, like Kardar think that the Indian cricket team is a 'Hindu' team, it is pertinent to mention that four of our Test captains have been Muslims—Iftikhar Ali Khan Pataudi, Ghulam Ahmed, Mansoor Ali Khan Pataudi and Mohammad Azharuddin. Other Indian cricket captains from minority communities have included such illustrious names as Vijay Samuel Hazare and Chandu Borde (Christians), Polly Umrigar and Nari Contractor (Parsis) and Bishen Singh Bedi (Sikh). Countless other non-Hindus have represented India in international cricket. As against this, only seven non-Muslims have done so for Pakistan, and just two of them—Anil Dalpat and Danish Kaneria have been Hindus.

I found that most Pakistanis viewed India as a Hindu country, and that they could not appreciate our monumental efforts to build not just a multi-religious cricket team, but also a secular nation. Minority communities are second class citizens in Pakistan, and even today most Pakistanis cannot grasp the fact that Muslims and other minorities in India enjoy equal status in all respects. During our conversations, we had to often enlighten Pakistanis about how well Indian Muslims were doing in all fields, as the controlled Pakistani media was always twisting facts and projecting the situation in India in a distorted and false manner.

Throughout my three and a half year stay in Pakistan, it was distressing to observe the anti-Hindu sentiments held so widely among the majority of Muslims there. This position seems to have only worsened with the passage of time. Hindus are regarded as *kaffirs*, and Islamic fundamentalist groups operating in the country freely distribute anti-Hindu propaganda material to the masses. Hindus are regularly accused of collaborating with foreigners against Pakistan.

In our conversations, some Pakistani Hindus would confide that their community members were subjected to pressure and intimidation by radical groups in order to force them to leave Pakistan. Hindu girls were often reportedly kidnapped and forcibly converted to Islam before being coerced into marrying Muslims. Attacks on temples, especially in the interior areas of Sindh, took place from time to time. The plight of Hindus has only worsened due to the rise of radicalised Islam in Pakistan.

I had many opportunities to discuss the plight of Pakistani Hindus and other minorities with Minocher (Minoo) Bhandara, who was President Zia's Advisor on Minorities. He was a prominent Parsee businessman and his family had owned a thriving liquor business for over a hundred years, including the famous Murree Brewery.

Minoo's family was not only financially well off but also intellectually oriented. His sister Bapsi Sidhwa is a well-known novelist known for her collaborative work with the film maker Deepa Mehta. Bapsi wrote *Ice Candy Man* on which the film *Earth* was made by Deepa Mehta, as well as the novel *Water* based on Deepa Mehta's movie by the same name.

Minoo's obituary written by his cousin, Ardeshir Cowasjee which was published in *The Dawn* on 22 June 2008 soon after his death made the following comment about him:

Minoo was Chief Executive of Muree Brewery since 1961. In 1981, he was appointed a member of Zia-ul-Haq's Majlis-e-Shoora, *serving as Advisor to the President of Pakistan on Minority Affairs, and this as a Parsee and a brewer to a President renowned for his-over-the-top religiosity. It is a measure of Minoo's gentle character and diplomacy that throughout the turbulent Talibanised years, he and his brewery survived and throve, as they have survived the local political* mullah's *and their nonsense.*[21]

Although the liquor business of the Bhandara family survived, it did go through a tough time after Bhutto banned the consumption of alcohol by Muslims, who constituted 97% of the population, and Zia's government enforced this ban with even greater fervour. Foreigners and members of Pakistan's minority communities were issued permits to enable them to purchase alcoholic beverages in limited quantities from designated shops. However, their numbers were so small that the turnover of the liquor businesses went down drastically.

Incidentally, I must describe a trend that had become rather common in Karachi. Many well-to-do Muslims would employ Hindus or Christians as domestic servants on condition that the latter would first hand over their liquor permits to them! These tipplers were thus able to circumvent the ban on sale of alcohol to Muslims being enforced by the authorities. Where there is a will, there is a way!

Minoo Bhandara was always rather tight-lipped about his role as Zia's Advisor on Minorities, but after a few glasses of Murree beer (made by his own brewery) he would open up. He was of the firm belief that Pakistan was not set up as a theocratic state, but rather as a secular one; he had no doubt communicated this to Zia. During one of our conversations, he recalled Jinnah's speech on 11 August 1947 when he presided over Pakistan's Constituent Assembly. Jinnah had said:

You are free to go to your temples, you are free to go to your mosques or to any other place of worship. You are free to belong to any religion or creed, and that has nothing to do with the business of the state.

Jinnah had also said: *"We are starting with the fundamental principle that we are all citizens and equal citizens of one state."*

Minoo was emphatic that Jinnah was clear in his belief that religion would be kept apart from temporal matters in Pakistan, for in the very same speech he had also said:

Now I think we should keep that in front of us that in course of time Hindus would cease to be Hindus and Muslims would cease to be

Muslims not in the religious sense, because that is the faith of each individual, but in the political sense as citizens of the state.

Minoo would also often refer to Jinnah's radio broadcast to the people of the United States in February 1948 in which he had categorically ruled out a theocracy:

In any case, Pakistan is not going to be a theocratic state to be ruled by priests with a divine vision. We have many non-Muslims— Hindus, Christians, Parsees—but they are all Pakistanis. They will enjoy the same rights and privileges as other citizens, and will play their rightful part in the affairs of Pakistan.

Although the Objectives Resolution of 1949 envisaged an official role for Islam as the state religion, Pakistan retained most of the laws that were inherited from the British secular legal code. It was only in 1956 that the name 'Islamic Republic of Pakistan' was adopted and Islam was officially declared the state religion. However, no simultaneous measures were taken to Islamise the legal system.

It was under Bhutto that the process of Islamisation received a fillip. He not only banned alcohol and gambling, but also declared the Ahmedia community to be non-Muslims.

Zia ul Haq took the Islamisation process to a whole different level during his rule from 1977-88. From this period onwards, the difficulties of the Hindu minority worsened considerably, with Islamic hardline groups unleashing a campaign of hatred and vendetta towards these hapless people. One Hindu businessman whom I knew rather well said to me, "Our life in twentieth century Pakistan is what it must have been like for Hindus during the rule of Allauddin Khilji, Aurangzeb or many other such tyrants who ruled over India," and lamented that "India does nothing to help us".

However, as the Islamisation process gathered momentum, so too did the opposition to it from some quarters. Minoo Bhandara was among the few who dared to question the government's Islamisation policies in the National Assembly. I cannot do better than to quote again from the obituary of Minoo Bhandara written by Ardeshir Cowasjee in *The Dawn.*[21]

On 12 Sept 2006, as a member of parliament from the ruling party, Minoo Bhandara moved a private bill, the subject of which was that mythical thing known as the 'ideology of Pakistan', asking his fellow parliamentarians to "Tell us what exactly is the ideology of our country...". He rightly observed that it was not reflected in the Objectives Resolution (a disaster from which this country has never recovered) which forms both the Preamble to the Constitution of Pakistan and its Annexe. The bill was naturally rejected as the honourable representatives of the people of Pakistan were not in unanimity as to what exactly is the ideology. They had their own varied interpretations but none wished a debate. Bhandara had made his point.

These people's representatives do not and cannot talk to each other; they merely talk at each other, make a lot of noise, thump their desks and then walk out. None have courage or convictions.

✦ ✦ ✦

Curriculum of hatred

XXIV

Compounding the problems for Hindus was the fact that hatred against them was being officially propagated through textbooks in Pakistan. The anti-Hindu bias got further strengthened on account of the fact that the public school curriculum was Islamised from the 1970s and has steadily adopted an anti-Hindu stance.

The three-and-a-half-year period of my stay in Karachi from December 1981 was exactly when under Zia ul Haq's directives, the revisionism of Pakistan's history was being implemented at a feverish pitch. Some of my Pakistani friends lamented that their children had to learn the textbooks by rote if they were to pass exams, and any disagreement in regard to the subject matter was punishable.

While the distortion of history attempted during Zia's rule was supported by the establishment, it provoked strong criticism as it progressed, among sections of scholars and the intelligentsia who were of the view that it promoted hatred and prejudice among students. While there were academics who strongly supported his efforts to usher in Islamic rule, there were also a large number who equally vehemently felt that his policies were resulting in the Talibanisation of the country. Pakistan was inevitably getting polarised on this as well as several other counts. The portents were that the wind that was gathering momentum during Zia's rule would become a gale and blow away Pakistan into an abyss of violence.

The noted historian and scholar Dr. Yvette Claire Rosser has written in her Ph.D dissertation *Curriculum as Destiny: Forging National Identity in India, Pakistan and Bangladesh* submitted to The University of Texas at Austin in 2003:

From their government-issued text books, students are taught that Hindus are backward, superstitious, they burn their widows and wives, and that Brahmins are inherently cruel, and if given a chance would exert their power over the weak, especially Muslims and Shudras, and would deprive them of education by pouring molten lead in their ears. In their Social Studies classes, students are taught that Islam brought peace, equality and justice to the sub-continent and only through Islam could the sinister ways of Hindus be held in check. In Pakistani textbooks 'Hindu' rarely appears in a sentence without adjectives such as politically astute, sly or manipulative.[22]

According to the historian Dr. Mubarak Ali, textbook 'reform' in Pakistan began with the introduction of Pakistan Studies and Islamic Studies by Zulfiqar Ali Bhutto in the early Seventies as a compulsory subject. From 1977 onwards, Zia ul Haq exploited this initiative and took the process of historical revisionism to an altogether different level. As Dr. Mubarak Ali put it:

The Pakistan establishment taught their children right from the beginning that this state was built on the basis of religion—that is why they don't have tolerance for other religions and want to wipe out all of them.[23]

In an editorial *Curriculum of Hatred* (20.5.2005), Pakistan's oldest and most respected newspaper *The Dawn* stated:

By propagating concepts such as jihad, the inferiority of non-Muslims, India's ingrained enmity with Pakistan, etc., the Text Book Board publications used by all government schools promote a mind-set that is bigoted and obscurantist. Since there are more children studying in these schools than in the 'madrassahs', the damage done is greater.[24]

The National Commission for Justice and Peace, a non-profit Catholic Church organisation in Pakistan has stated in a report published in 2005 that textbooks in Pakistan have been used to create hatred towards Hindus, and that through these textbooks Pakistani students are taught that Hindus are backward and superstitious. The report further states:

Textbooks reflect intentional obfuscation. Today's students, citizens of Pakistan and its future leaders are the victims of these partial lies.[25]

In 2003, The Sustainable Development Policy Institute, an Islamabad-based think tank released a report based on a survey of Pakistani Social Studies, Civics, Urdu and English textbooks. It pointed out the inaccurate facts and omissions in these textbooks which distorted the significance of actual events. The report asserts:

Associated with the insistence on the ideology of Pakistan has been an essential component of hate against India and the Hindus. For the upholders of the ideology of Pakistan, the existence of Pakistan is defined only in relation to Hindus, and hence the Hindus have to be painted as negatively as possible.[26]

The report continues by stating:

The distortion of history has increasingly warped Pakistan's view both of self and others for decades. Each generation has twisted the facts that it passes to the next. This has served to create a world view that is removed from reality and confounds efforts to understand and fully resolve important social, national and international problems.

Four themes emerge most strongly as constituting the bulk of the curricula and textbooks of the three compulsory subjects: That Pakistan is for Muslims alone; that Islamiat *is to be forcibly taught to all students; that the Ideology of Pakistan is to be internationalised as faith and hate is to be created against Hindus and India; and students are to be encouraged to take the path of* jihad *and* shahadat *(martyrdom).*

Analysing these trends, the eminent Indian journalist and writer BG Verghese hit the nail on the head when he made an observation about Pakistan in an article *Myth and hate as history* which appeared in *The Hindu* on 23.6.2004:

It has yet to come to terms with its identity and rich plurality, shared history and composite culture which it needs to internalise. The 'ideology of Pakistan' to which it clings has to be something more than the ruling military-cum-religious right credo of hate for the Indian/ Hindu 'other' that informs textbook policy.[27]

He makes the pertinent comment:

The term ideology of Pakistan first enunciated in 1962, gained currency under Zia. However, it has been officially fathered on Jinnah, who actually spoke of a liberal, pluralistic Pakistan in his inaugural address to the nation's Constituent Assembly on 11 August, 1947. The imagined history of Pakistan, as officially taught, names Mohammad bin Qasim as the first citizen of Pakistan and father of the Pakistan movement. MD Zafar's Text Book of Pakistan Studies even affirms that 'except for its name, the present-day Pakistan has existed as more or less a single entity for centuries'. There is amnesia regarding the creation of Bangladesh and other uncomfortable facts.

✦ ✦ ✦

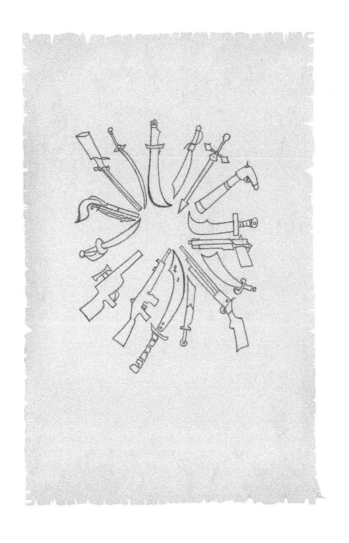

A picture is worth a thousand words

XXV

I left Karachi on transfer to New Delhi in May 1985. During the three decades which have elapsed since then, a lot of water has flowed down the Indus River but tragically, a lot of blood has also been spilt on Pakistan's streets and alleys.

The descent into unbridled violence has been too well chronicled to need reiteration. However, it is pertinent to mention that the violence has taken many forms—religious, sectarian and ethnic.

Religious violence has targeted not only Hindus, but also Christians and Ahmadis as well. All these minorities have been traumatised beyond description, and there seems to be no relief in sight for them.

Sectarian violence has also flared up with great regularity between the Sunni majority and the Shia minority. Human Rights Watch estimates that thousands of Shias have been killed in attacks by Sunni extremists. Such attacks have often targeted worshipers at Shia mosques. Shias constitute around 21% of Pakistan's population while the Sunnis are over 75%.

The Shia-Sunni sectarian violence in Pakistan has dangerous dimensions because it could become an extension of the wider conflict raging in many parts of West Asia, including Iraq, Syria and Yemen. Pakistan faces the prospect of becoming another full scale battle ground for the raging proxy war between Iran on one hand, and Saudi Arabia along with the other Gulf Arab states on the other.

In May 2015 came the tragic news about an attack in Karachi by pistol-wielding men on a bus carrying members of the Shia Ismaili sect who are followers of the Agha Khan. At least 43 people were killed in the incident, which was the first in Pakistan for which the Islamic State has claimed responsibility. There are many other indications of the growing footprint of the Islamic State in Pakistan, and this is bound to have ramifications for the Shia minority.

Ethnic violence has erupted time and again between the various constituent groups in Pakistan. Being a melting pot of various ethnic groups, Karachi has witnessed more such violence than other cities in the country. During my stay in Karachi in the early eighties, I witnessed how the situation there was becoming explosive, with tensions mounting between the Sindhis and *Muhajirs*. Since the mid-1980s, more than 3000 persons are estimated to have died in hostilities between them. Other communities such as the Pathans, Punjabis and Balochis have also got engulfed in the fighting which has become more and more rampant. By the turn of the century, Karachi had already become a sort of Beirut, and street fighting and violence between different ethnic groups kept spiralling.

At the time of my transfer from Pakistan in 1985, the country had begun to crawl back to a semblance of Parliamentary government, and people had started becoming hopeful that their lives would now start returning to normal. Their hopes were completely belied. The seeds of violence had already been sown in the body politic and Pakistan was destined to face the consequences.

Three years later, on 17 August 1988, President Zia along with several high ranking military and civilian officials was killed in a plane crash near Bahawalpur. The US Ambassador to Pakistan, Arnold Raphael was also killed in that accident. The plane carrying them plunged from the sky and hit the ground with such force that the wreckage got scattered over a vast area. An 11-year long deeply divisive phase in Pakistan's history came to an end in this tragic manner.

Zia's body-parts were never found after his plane exploded. A Pakistani journalist who described the plane crash to me a few days later quipped: "President Zia—may he rest in pieces."

K Natwar Singh, Minister of State and former Ambassador to Pakistan attended the funeral as a member of the Indian delegation led by President Venkataraman. He wrote later in an article: *The crowd was enormous but the coffin was almost empty.*[28]

According to some sources, the coffin contained only Zia's spectacles, jawbone and false teeth.

I feel saddened by the fact that our Consulate, which was widely commended in Karachi for exemplary public service, had to be closed down in December 1994 and has not been reopened since.

Earlier, in a horrific incident indicating the rapidly deteriorating bilateral relationship, the Consul General's residence had been attacked and ransacked by a violent mob in December 1992. Part of the residence was burnt, and the Consul General's family managed to escape disaster by hiding in a bathroom.

Situated across the road from the Consul General's residence, Bhutto House is said to have a curse on it. Zulfiqar Ali Bhutto, the man who built it was hanged in April 1979; his eldest child Benazir was assassinated in December 2007; his elder son Murtaza was killed in a police encounter near this very house in September 1996, while his younger son died earlier in mysterious circumstances in Nice, France in July 1986. Bhutto House bears testimony to how the trappings of power in Pakistan can be soaked in so much blood.

When will the desert bloom?

Epilogue

Amidst all the turbulence which has marked Pakistan's sixty eight-year history, and which has seen civilian governments and military juntas play musical chairs with one another, one aspect that has retained the stamp of permanence has been its unremitting hostility towards India and its steadfast desire to foment trouble across its eastern border. The inevitable conclusion that is drawn in India is that the ill-will of the Pakistan establishment, especially that of the army cannot be transformed into goodwill; whenever Pakistan can create problems for us, it will always do so. In turn, this has given rise to anti-Pakistan sentiments in many sections of Indian society.

Given the fact that Pakistan's economic, industrial and military strength is considerably less than India's, a fundamental plank of its policy continues to be built around the asymmetric or proxy war involving the sending of terrorists across the Line of Control. In an interview with *Dunya News* on 25 October 2015, former President Pervez Musharraf has himself admitted that since the 1990's Pakistani forces had trained groups like Lashkar-e-Taiba to carry out militancy in Kashmir. Although the Line of Control is fenced, there are portions of it where rivers and rivulets make the fencing vulnerable and such sections are used by the infiltrators.

On 29 September 2015 while speaking at the UN General Assembly Pakistan's Prime Minister Nawaz Sharif put forward a four-point proposal which inter alia included the following:

1) *Complete cease fire by India and Pakistan along the Line of Control;*

2) *Reaffirmation by both sides that they will not resort to the threat or use of force under any circumstances;*

3) *De-militarisation of Kashmir; and*

4) *An unconditional withdrawal by both sides from the Siachen Glacier, the world's highest battleground.*

At face value, the four-point proposal may appear eminently reasonable, but a closer analysis would show that its acceptance by India would in fact make it easier for Pakistan to continue waging proxy war, as it will pave the way for terrorists to infiltrate more easily from the Pakistani side and create mayhem across the Line of Control.

Points 1) and 2) would simply ensure that Indian forces will not be able to fire at these terrorists when they cross the Line of Control.

Point 3) would mean that with Kashmir de-militarised, the Indian army would not be there to check-mate the plans of these terrorists.

Point 4) would mean that once India vacates the Siachen Glacier, Pakistan would have a chance to occupy it sometime in the future and secure that strategic advantage which it was prevented from having since 1984. As in other instances,

Pakistan would claim that these occupiers were not its own troops but 'Kashmiri freedom fighters'.

Like Zia's *No War Pact*, Sharif's proposal too does not address India's concerns about terrorism nor put an end to the proxy war that seems to be escalating and gathering momentum. The Indian army has exercised restraint but unending Pakistani provocations compel it to pursue a more aggressive approach. Recently, it lifted a self-imposed restriction on bringing in artillery, thus forcing Pakistan to tone down its belligerence.[29]

A complicating factor of course, is that both India and Pakistan are nuclear weapon states. Pakistan has repeatedly threatened that it would use nuclear weapons if it feels the need to do so. This does not augur well for the future, as the destruction that could result from a war involving the use of nuclear weapons by both sides is unimaginable.

Pakistan's National Security Adviser Sartaj Aziz said recently in August 2015 that India should not take his country for granted, adding, "Pakistan has nuclear weapons." In July 2015, Pakistan's Defence Minister Asif Khawaja said "We pray that such an option never arises, but if we need to use them (nuclear weapons) for our survival, we will." Pervez Musharraf had also said (after leaving his office): "We do not want to use nuclear capability but if our existence comes under threat, what do we have these weapons for?"

A fresh threat was made recently by Pakistan's Foreign Secretary Aijaz Choudhary when he said on 20 October 2015 that his country had developed low yield nuclear weapons which would be used against Indian troops if conventional war broke out.

Many Indian analysts feel that these threats are only a bluff, for Pakistan knows fully well that a retaliatory Indian nuclear strike would destroy it completely. Nevertheless, in such a scenario, an agreement on Non-First Use of Nuclear Weapons is absolutely necessary if the possibility of incalculable mutual destruction is to be prevented, even if such a possibility is considered miniscule.

Not surprisingly, Pakistan is unwilling to enter into such an agreement. Its game plan is to continue sending terrorists across the Line of Control and to threaten that it will use nuclear weapons if any retaliatory Indian action endangers its security. It is evident that the threat of first use of nuclear weapons is fundamental to this strategy.

Both India and Pakistan have a wealth of human and other resources, but unfortunately they are not able to realise their true potential due to the unending conflict. The bigger casualty of this conflict are the Pakistanis.

The Pakistani writer Iftikhar Tariq Khanzada has summed up his country's plight in an article entitled *Pakistan: A Failed State*, which appeared in *Liberty Voice* on 22 January 2014:

The feudal-military-mullah nexus has ruled the country for the majority of its history. This is the main reason that democracy, which is flourishing across the border, has not been able to establish its credentials here. Over 60 percent of Pakistan's GDP goes towards

meeting its defense needs, consequently the overall economy suffers.
Education in Pakistan has never been a priority with any
government, so has been the case with social security and well-being of
its citizens. Rampant inflation, unemployment, the daily deepening
energy crises, unchecked corruption and the alarming, deteriorating
law and order situation have made Pakistan a favorite recruiting
ground plus a safe haven for terrorists from all over the world. It did
not come as a surprise that Osama Bin Laden was found living in
Abbottabad Cantonment in the failed state of Pakistan.

It is the Pakistanis themselves who have to rectify the bizarre
situation that exists in their country, though it will be a long
haul for them. Until the stranglehold of the feudal-military-
mullah nexus weakens, Pakistan's policy towards India will
continue to be extremely hostile.

In this scenario, hoping for a quick turn-around in Indo-
Pakistan relations may just be wishful thinking. Perhaps it is,
but I must admit that I have secretly indulged in it since 1978
when I went to Egypt on my first diplomatic posting and
witnessed Anwar Sadat and Menachem Begin bury the hatchet
between their two countries. Egypt and Israel, too had fought
deadly wars in 1948, 1967 and 1973, but there is peace between
them now, even though some people refer to it as 'a cold peace'.

It cannot be emphasised enough how important it is to end the
deeply ingrained hostility unless we want to risk hurtling
towards another conflict, one that will perhaps be more
destructive than any in the past. We need bold and out-of-the-

box thinking to chart out a new course. To use a cliché, the bull has to be taken by the horns.

Instead of refusing to hold talks, we should show willingness to talk at all times and discuss all issues threadbare. We have a 'back channel' which is believed to be quite active. It is now time to put the 'front channel' in high gear. This is without doubt India's thorniest relationship, and it needs a bold initiative from the very top.

In this regard, the recent meeting of India's National Security Adviser Ajit Doval with Pakistan's new National Security Adviser Lt. Gen. (Retired) Nasir Janjua which was held in Bangkok on 6th December 2015 is a signal that the Prime Ministers of the two countries have taken the initiative to not only resume the stalled dialogue but to make it unconditional and cover the entire range of issues which bedevil the bilateral relationship.

Prime Minister Modi has reached out to audiences all over the world, and it is heartening to note that he will be going to Pakistan in 2016 for the SAARC Summit. During his visit, which will be mainly for promoting regional cooperation, it may be useful to also reach out to the people of Pakistan and unequivocally convey the message that we want cordial, cooperative and friendly relations.

Regardless of his rhetoric that is often strident, Nawaz Sharif is someone who wants to rein in his army, and who could thus play a role in changing the tenor of the Indo-Pakistan relationship.

It is true that Prime Minister Vajpayee's goodwill Lahore bus trip was followed by Pakistan's Kargil misadventure, but Sharif has been at pains to emphasise that he was kept in the dark about the military operations till they were in full swing, and we should give him the benefit of doubt.

Can Sharif break free from the shackles of the armed forces? It would not be easy for him, but we must take our chances; an elected head of government in Pakistan would at least have the moral authority to chart a new course, unlike a Zia or a Musharraf.

If a handshake between Modi and Nawaz Sharif sends out reassuring signals, one can imagine what a bear hug by them would do. Atmospherics are very important in diplomacy. At present, the Indo-Pakistan atmospherics are awful. Nothing positive can emerge when the atmosphere is so vitiated and rife with mutual suspicion.

When the relationship is plagued by so many problems, it is not asking for too much that the Prime Ministers of India and Pakistan hold summit meetings periodically in order to resolve differences. Other ministers such as those dealing with foreign affairs, home/interior, commerce, industry, energy, health and education should also meet frequently so that an agenda for cooperation can begin to take centre stage. The naysayers will be dismissive of this, but what do we have to lose by trying?

Will we ever be able to resolve what Pakistan regards as the core issue – the Kashmir dispute? It is very difficult, but I would not say that it is impossible. It may be pertinent to note that according to the reputed journalist Kuldip Nayyar, Nawaz Sharif had himself admitted to him some years ago that neither can Pakistan take away Kashmir from India nor can India give it away.[30]

Some analysts have suggested that the only reasonable and workable solution is to eschew jingoism and settle the Kashmir dispute by recognising the Line of Control as an International Border. They feel that this is the only alternative to the endless hostility which only impoverishes both countries.

In his treatise *Securing India's future in the new millennium*, the well-known strategic analyst Brahma Chellaney has opined:

In the long run, the only possible solution to the Kashmir dispute is for the three countries (India, Pakistan and China) to let bygones be bygones and agree to be content with the J&K territories they control.[31]

In a similar vein, US Ambassadors Teresita Schaffer and Howard Schaffer (both of whom have considerable experience of serving in South Asian countries) wrote in an article in the *International Herald Tribune*:

All three countries (India, Pakistan and China) have nuclear weapons and are politically attached to their territorial claims. The chances of peaceful territorial adjustments are therefore nil, and the dangers of territorial adjustment by war too horrible to contemplate. The answer is a freeze. This means turning the India-Pakistan Line of Control and the current India-China Line of Actual Control into recognised international borders, and giving final recognition to the China-Pakistan border settlement that India disputes.[32]

Andrew C. Winner and Toshi Yoshihara have also suggested in their article: *India and Pakistan at the Edge*:

As a key part of the move towards a permanent settlement, the United States-- and ideally the other permanent members of the Security Council –should express their willingness to recognise the line of control as the international border between the two countries.[33]

A starting point could be to discuss the lacunae in Sharif's four-point proposal and work out a formulation acceptable to both countries. Proceeding from there, we can try to work towards an overall settlement in due course. The undeniable fact is that Indo-Pakistan relations can only be set right through a spirit of give and take; if the willingness to compromise is absent, then the hostility will keep increasing.

Of course, there can be no watering down of our demand that the nurseries of terrorism in Pakistan have to be closed down. Hopefully, Pakistan will begin to realise that its policy of sponsoring terrorism is causing great damage to itself, as thousands of Pakistanis have died in acts of terrorism committed by the very same outfits which have been trained by the ISI and the armed forces; after all, chickens do come home to roost.

Kashmiri separatists also have to understand that independence for Jammu and Kashmir is out of the question, and that securing more autonomy within the Indian Constitution could be the most they can hope for.

It may take a very long time for everything to fall in place; there will be numerous set-backs. However, gradually working towards this objective is preferable to just being reconciled to the war of attrition.

As a first step, the process of instilling hatred among the youth through textbooks should end as hatred only begets hatred. School textbooks in both countries should be carefully sanitised to eliminate any sort of hate mongering. There are enough right-minded people in both countries who want this to be done. Wars begin in the minds of people, and children in Pakistan and India should not grow up perceiving each other as enemies whom they want to annihilate.

Another immediate step should be to rein in extremist groups that fan hatred. This may sound daunting, but where there is a will, there is a way.

Widening people to people contacts is also necessary in order to reduce the hostility. We should play not only cricket but all sports with each other. We should welcome Pakistan's musicians, artists, intellectuals, writers and people from different walks of society and encourage it to welcome ours. Rather than allow politics to encroach into these areas, we should chart a course whereby an across-the-board interaction lowers the temperature of political hostility. In any case, we should not fall prey to bigotry, prejudice or hate-mongering as this only serves the agenda of those in Pakistan who preach hatred against India.

The US too must wake up to reality and realise the folly of leaning so heavily on Pakistan's Generals as this ends up strengthening the latter's role in domestic politics and has detrimental consequences for the forces of democracy. Supporting the forces of democracy has been important for the Americans in Iraq and Syria, and so should it be in Pakistan too. A challenge for Indian diplomacy is to drive home the point that these Generals and the *mullahs* have collaborated to set up those infamous nurseries of terrorism which are principally intended to target India but will also strike at anyone perceived to be an enemy of Islam, including the Americans themselves.

Many in India as well as in Pakistan hope that one day our countries could live together as prosperous, good neighbours, much as France and Germany do now after having endured centuries of mutual conflicts. They hark back to those days when the Indian sub-continent produced so much wealth that it was called *sone ki chidiya* (a bird made of gold).

That bird is now malnourished, sick and weak. The IMF rankings of countries in terms of Per Capita Income (2014) places India at 125 in the list and Pakistan at 135 with figures of US$ 5808 and US $ 4749, respectively. By comparison, Malaysia is ranked at 47 with US$ 25145, Thailand at 76 with US$ 15579, Indonesia at 102 with US$ 10651 and Sri Lanka at 103 with US $ 10410. Only really underdeveloped countries rank behind the South Asian giants India and Pakistan. Despite the fact that the South Asian Association for Regional Cooperation (SAARC) has been in existence since December 1985, it has precious little to show by way of real cooperation unlike ASEAN, another regional cooperation organisation in Asia.

It is an axiomatic truth that our region needs not conflict but development. To continue on our present path would be catastrophic. By working together, we can usher in a new age filled with hope not just for the two countries but for the whole of South Asia.

I cannot do better than convey my hopes in the words of Faiz Ahmed Faiz who is adored in Pakistan as well as in and India:

Gulon mein rang bhare, baad-e-naubahar chale.

(The blossoms are filled with colours, a new spring breeze blows).

I have waited in vain for this breeze, and it is unlikely to start blowing anytime soon. However, I hope that it does blow sometime in the future, filling the arid, thorny landscape of the India-Pakistan relationship with colourful flowers.

References

1) William Burr's report *New documents spotlight Reagan Era tensions over Pakistani nuclear programme* published by the Wilson Center, April 25, 2012.

2) US Embassy Pakistan cable 10239 dated 5 July 1982 to State Department, Digital Archive, Wilson Center.

3) Chapter VII, *The Kao-boys of R&AW* by B Raman.

4) *Pakistan, Zia and After*, Anthony Hyman, Mohammad Ghayur and Naresh Kaushik (page 36).

5) *Pakistan's Mango Diplomacy Hit by Insect Fear*, Dr. Ranga Kalansooriya, *Colombo Telegraph*, 31 July 2013.

6) Wikipedia.

7) *The Heart's Filthy Lesson*, Nadeem Paracha, *The Dawn*, 14 February 2014.

8) BBC News, 26 September 1998. Report by Owen Bennet Jones.

9) Faiz' acceptance speech, Lenin Peace Prize Ceremony, 1962.

10) *Ahmed Faraz, outspoken Urdu poet dies at 77*, Haresh Pandya, *New York Times*, 1 September 2008.

11) *General Ali Kuli refutes Musharraf's narrative*, Rahimullah Yusufzai, *The News*, 5 October 2006.

12) *Pakistan: Diplomatic Cross-fire*, Dilip Bobb, *India Today*, February 15, 1982.

13) CNN iReport, March 23, 2014.

14) *We only receive back the bodies*, article on Balochistan in *The Economist*, 7 August 2012.

15) *Holi's home*, Haroon Khalid in *Friday Times*, 15-21 April 2011.

16) Page 264, *Indian Cricket Controversies* KR Wadhwaney.

17) Suvajit Mustafi, *Criclife*, 30 January 2015.

18) *Shadows Across the Playing Fields,* Shashi Tharoor and Shahryar Khan.

19) *The Infamous Shakoor Rana- Mike Gatting Altercation*, Arunabha Sengupta in *Cricket Country*, 7 December 2012.

20) *Reverse Sweeps: Pakistan's crazy cricket controversies*, Nadeem Paracha, *The Dawn*, 19 June, 2013.

21) *A Master Brewer*, Ardeshir Cowasjee, *The Dawn*, 22 June 2008.

22) *Curriculum as Destiny: Forging National Identity in India, Pakistan and Bangladesh*, Dr. Yvette Claire Rosser.

23) *The threat of Pakistan's revisionist texts*, Afnan Khan, *The Guardian*, 18 May 2009.

24) *Curriculum of hatred*, editorial in *The Dawn*, May 20, 2009.

25) Report in *Daily Times*, Pakistan, April 25, 2006.

26) *The Subtle Subversion*, a report by the Sustainable Development Institute, Islamabad. (Editors: AH Nayyar and Ahmad Salim).

27) *Myth and hate as history*, by BG Verghese, *The Hindu*, 23 June 2004.

28) *What does Pakistan have about which India should be making such a noise, Rediff on the net,* Special by K Natwar Singh.

29) *Army brings in Artillery for LOC fight, ready to 'shock' Pakistan,* report by Rahul Singh in *The Hindustan Times*, October 10, 2015.

30) *Kashmir can never be taken nor given, Nawaz Sharif told me: Kuldip Nayyar,* PTI report, 25 July 2015.

31) *Securing India's future in the new millennium*, Brahma Chellaney.

32) *Freeze Himalayan borders before fighting escalates,* Teresita C. Schaffer and Howard B. Schaffer in *International Herald Tribune*, 15 June 1999.

33) *India and Pakistan at the Edge*, Andrew C. Winner and Toshi Yoshihara in the IISS Quarterly Journal *Survival*, Volume 44 Number 3 page 74.

Lightning Source UK Ltd.
Milton Keynes UK
UKHW010627100422
401340UK00001B/274

9 789385 020322